# The Flood
# The Miller's Daughter,
# Captain Burle,
# Death of Olivier Becaille

by

# Emile Zola

The Echo Library 2007

Published by

The Echo Library

Echo Library
131 High St.
Teddington
Middlesex TW11 8HH

www.echo-library.com

Please report serious faults in the text to complaints@echo-library.com

ISBN 978-1-40688-018-2

# Contents

# THE FLOOD

## I.

My name is Louis Roubien. I am seventy years old. I was born in the village of Saint-Jory, several miles up the Garonne from Toulouse.

For fourteen years I battled with the earth for my daily bread. At last, prosperity smiled on we, and last month I was still the richest farmer in the parish.

Our house seemed blessed, happiness reigned there. The sun was our brother, and I cannot recall a bad crop. We were almost a dozen on the farm. There was myself, still hale and hearty, leading the children to work; then my young brother, Pierre, an old bachelor and retired sergeant; then my sister, Agathe, who came to us after the death of her husband. She was a commanding woman, enormous and gay, whose laugh could be heard at the other end of the village. Then came all the brood: my son, Jacques; his wife, Rosie, and their three daughters, Aimee, Veronique, and Marie. The first named was married to Cyprica Bouisson, a big jolly fellow, by whom she had two children, one two years old and the other ten months. Veronique was just betrothed, and was soon to marry Gaspard Rabuteau. The third, Marie, was a real young lady, so white, so fair, that she looked as if born in the city.

That made ten, counting everybody. I was a grandfather and a great-grandfather. When we were at table I had my sister, Agathe, at my right, and my brother, Pierre, at my left. The children formed a circle, seated according to age, with the heads diminishing down to the baby of ten months, who already ate his soup like a man. And let me tell you that the spoons in the plates made a clatter. The brood had hearty appetites. And what gayety between the mouthfuls! I was filled with pride and joy when the little ones held out their hands toward me, crying:

"Grandpa, give us some bread! A big piece, grandpa!"

Oh! the good days! Our farm sang from every corner. In the evening, Pierre invented games and related stories of his regiment. On Sunday Agathe made cakes for the girls. Marie knew some canticles, which she sang like a chorister. She looked like a saint, with her blond hair falling on her neck and her hands folded on her apron.

I had built another story on the house when Aimee had married Cyprien; and I said laughingly that I would have to build another after the wedding of Veronique and Gaspard. We never cared to leave each other. We would sooner have built a city behind the farm, in our enclosure. When families are united, it is so good to live and die where one has grown up!

The month of May had been magnificent that year. It was long since the crops gave such good promise. That day precisely, I had made a tour of inspection with my son, Jacques. We started at about three o'clock. Our meadows on the banks of the Garonne were of a tender green. The grass was three feet high, and an osier thicket, planted the year before, had sprouts a yard high. From there we went to visit our wheat and our vines, fields bought one by one as fortune came to us. The wheat was growing strong; the vines, in full flower, promised a superb vintage. And Jacques laughed his good laugh as he slapped me on the shoulder.

"Well, father, we shall never want for bread nor for wine. You must be a friend of the Divine Power to have silver showered upon your land in this way."

We often joked among ourselves of our past poverty. Jacques was right. I must have gained the friendship of some saint or of God himself, for all the luck in the country was for us. When it hailed the hail ceased on the border of our fields. If the vines of our neighbors fell sick, ours seemed to have a wall of protection around them. And in the end I grew to consider it only just. Never doing harm to any one, I thought that happiness was my due.

As we approached the house, Rose gesticulated, calling out:

"Hurry up!"

One of our cows had just had a calf, and everybody was excited. The birth of that little beast seemed one more blessing. We had been obliged recently to enlarge the stables, where we had nearly one hundred head of animals—cows and sheep, without counting the horses.

"Well, a good day's work!" I cried. "We will drink to-night a bottle of ripened wine."

Meanwhile, Rose took us aside and told us that Gaspard, Veronique's betrothed, had come to arrange the day for the wedding. She had invited him to remain for dinner.

Gaspard, the oldest son of a farmer of Moranges, was a big boy of twenty years, known throughout the country for his prodigious strength. During a festival at Toulouse he had vanquished Martial, the "Lion of the Midi." With that, a nice boy, with a heart of gold. He was even timid, and he blushed when Veronique looked him squarely in the face.

I told Rose to call him. He was at the bottom of the yard, helping our servants to spread out the freshly-washed linen. When he entered the dining room, where we were, Jacques turned toward me, saying:

"You speak, father."

"Well," I said, "you have come, my boy, to have us set the great day?"

"Yes, that is it, Father Roubien," he answered, very red.

"You mustn't blush, my boy," I continued. "It will be, if you wish, on Saint-Felicite day, the 10th of July. This is the 23rd of June, so you will have only twenty days to wait. My poor dead wife was called Felicite, and that will bring you happiness. Well? Is it understood?"

"Yes, that will do—Sainte-Felicite day. Father Roubien."

And he gave each of us a grip that made us wince. Then he embraced Rose, calling her mother. This big boy with the terrific fists loved Veronique to the point of losing his appetite.

Now," I continued, "you must remain for dinner. Well, everybody to the table. I have a thundering appetite, I have."

That evening we were eleven at table. Gaspard was placed next to Veronique, and he sat looking at her, forgetting his plate, so moved at the thought of her belonging to him that, at times, the tears sprang to his eyes. Cyprien and Aimee, married only three years, smiled. Jacques and Rose, who had had twenty-five years of married life, were more serious, but, surreptitiously, they exchanged tender glances. As for me, I seemed to relive in those two sweethearts, whose happiness seemed to bring a corner of Paradise to our table. What good soup we had that evening! Aunt Agathe, always ready with a witticism, risked several jokes. Then that honest Pierre wanted to relate his love affair with a young lady of Lyons. Fortunately, we were at the dessert, and every one was talking at once. I had brought two bottles of mellowed wine from the cellar. We drank to the good fortune of Gaspard and Veronique. Then we had singing. Gaspard knew some love songs in dialect. We also asked Marie for a canticle. She stood up and sang in a flute-like voice that tickled one's ears.

I went to the window, and Gaspard joined me there.

"Is there no news up your way?" I asked him.

"No," he answered. "There is considerable talk about the heavy rains of the last few days. Some seem to think that they will cause trouble."

In effect, it had rained for sixty hours without stopping. The Garonne was very much swollen since the preceding day, but we had confidence in it, and, as long as it did not overflow its banks, we could not look on it as a bad neighbor.

"Bah!" I exclaimed, shrugging my shoulders. "Nothing will happen. It is the same every year. The river puts up her back as if she were furious, and she calms down in a night. You will see, my boy, that it will amount to nothing this time. See how beautiful the weather is!"

And I pointed to the sky. It was seven o'clock; the sun was setting. The sky was blue, an immense blue sheet of profound purity, in which the rays of the setting sun were like a golden dust. Never had I seen the village drowsing in so sweet a peace. Upon the tiled roofs a rosy tint was fading. I heard a neighbor's laugh, then the voices of children at the turn in the road in front of our place. Farther away and softened by the distance, rose the sounds of flocks entering their sheds. The great voice of the Garonne roared continually; but it was to me as the voice of the silence, so accustomed to it was I.

Little by little the sky paled; the village became more drowsy. It was the evening of a beautiful day; and I thought that all our good fortune—the big harvests, the happy house, the betrothal of Veronique—came to us from above in the purity of the dying light. A benediction spread over us with the farewell of the evening.

Meanwhile I had returned to the center of the room. The girls were chattering. We listened to them, smiling. Suddenly, across the serenity of the country, a terrible cry sounded, a cry of distress and death:

"The Garonne! The Garonne!"

## II.

We rushed out into the yard.

Saint-Jory is situated at the bottom of a slope at about five hundred yards from the Garonne. Screens of tall poplars that divide the meadows, hide the river completely.

We could see nothing. And still the cry rang out:

"The Garonne! The Garonne!"

Suddenly, on the wide road before us, appeared two men and three women, one of them holding a child in her arms. It was they who were crying out, distracted, running with long strides. They turned at times, looking behind with terrified faces, as if a band of wolves was pursuing them.

"What's the matter with them?" demanded Cyprien. "Do you see anything, grandfather?"

"No," I answered. "The leaves are not even moving."

I was still talking when an exclamation burst from us. Behind the fugitives there appeared, between the trunks of the poplars, amongst the large tufts of grass, what looked like a pack of gray beasts speckled with yellow. They sprang up from all directions, waves crowding waves, a helter-skelter of masses of foaming water, shaking the sod with the rumbling gallop of their hordes.

It was our turn to send forth the despairing cry:

"The Garonne! The Garonne!"

The two men and the three women were still running on the road. They heard the terrible gallop gaining on them. Now the waves arrived in a single line, rolling, tumbling with the thunder of a charging battalion. With their first shock they had broken three poplars; the tall foliage sank and disappeared. A wooden cabin was swallowed up, a wall was demolished; heavy carts were carried away like straws. But the water seemed, above all, to pursue the fugitives. At the bend in the road, where there was a steep slope, it fell suddenly in an immense sheet and cut off retreat. They continued to run, nevertheless, splashing through the water, no longer shouting, mad with terror. The water swirled about their knees. An enormous wave felled the woman who was carrying the child. Then all were engulfed.

"Quick! Quick!" I cried. "We must get into the house. It is solid—we have nothing to fear."

We took refuge upstairs. The house was built on a hillock above the road. The water invaded the yard, softly, with a little rippling noise. We were not much frightened.

"Bah!" said Jacques, to reassure every one, "this will not amount to anything. You remember, father, in '55, the water came up into the yard. It was a foot deep. Then it receded."

"It is disastrous for the crops, just the same," murmured Cyprien.

"No, it will not be anything," I said, seeing the large questioning eyes of our girls.

Aimee had put her two children into the bed. She sat beside them, with Veronique and Marie. Aunt Agathe spoke of heating some wine she had brought up, to give us courage.

Jacques and Rose were looking out of a window. I was at the other, with my brother Pierre, Cyprien and Gaspard.

"Come up!" I cried to our two servants, who were wading in the yard. "Don't stay there and get all wet."

"But the animals?" they asked. "They are afraid. They are killing each other in the barn."

"No, no; come up! After a while we'll see to them."

The rescue of the animals would be impossible, if the disaster was to attain greater proportions. I thought it unnecessary to frighten the family. So I forced myself to appear hopeful. Leaning on the windowsill, I indicated the progress of the flood. The river, after its attack on the village, was in possession even to the narrowest streets. It was no longer a galloping charge, but a slow and invincible strangulation. The hollow in the bottom of which Saint-Jory is built was changed into a lake. In our yard the water was soon three feet deep. But I asserted that it remained stationary—I even went so far as to pretend that it was going down.

"Well, you will be obliged to sleep here to-night, my boy," I said, turning to Gaspard. "That is, unless the roads are free in a couple of hours—which is quite possible."

He looked at me without answering, his face quite pale; and I saw him look at Veronique with an expression of anguish.

It was half-past eight o'clock. It was still daylight—a pale, sad light beneath the blanched sky. The servants had had the forethought to bring up two lamps with them. I had them lighted, thinking that they would brighten up the somber room. Aunt Agathe, who had rolled a table to the middle of the room, wished to organize a card party. The worthy woman, whose eyes sought mine momentarily, thought above all of diverting the children. Her good humor kept up a superb bravery; and she laughed to combat the terror that she felt growing around her. She forcibly placed Aimee, Veronique, and Marie at the table. She put the cards into their hands, took a hand herself with an air of intense interest, shuffling, cutting, dealing with such a flow of talk that she almost drowned the noise of the water. But our girls could not be diverted; they were pale, with feverish hands, and ears on the alert. Every few moments there was a pause in the play. One of them would turn to me, asking in a low voice:

"Grandpa, is it still rising?"

"No, no. Go on with the game. There is no danger."

Never had my heart been gripped by such agony. All the men placed themselves at the windows to hide the terrifying sight. We tried to smile, turned toward the peaceful lamps that threw discs of light upon the table. I recalled our winter evenings, when we gathered around the table. It was the same quiet interior, filled with the warmth of affection. And while peace was there I heard behind me the roaring of the escaped river, that was constantly rising.

"Louis," said my brother Pierre, "the water is within three feet of the window. We ought to tell them."

I hushed him up by pressing his arm. But it was no longer possible to hide the peril. In our barns the animals were killing each other. There were bleatings and bellowings from the crazed herds; and the horses gave the harsh cries that can be heard at great distances when they are in danger of death.

"My God! My God!" cried Aimee, who stood up, pressing her hands to her temples.

They all ran to the windows. There they remained, mute, their hair rising with fear. A dim light floated above the yellow sheet of water. The pale sky looked like a white cloth thrown over the earth. In the distance trailed some smoke. Everything was misty. It was the terrified end of a day melting into a night of death. And not a human sound, nothing but the roaring of that sea stretching to infinity; nothing but the bellowings and the neighings of the animals.

"My God! My God!" repeated the women, in low voices, as if they feared to speak aloud.

A terrible cracking silenced the exclamations. The maddened animals had burst open the doors of the stables. They passed in the yellow flood, rolled about, carried away by the current. The sheep were tossed about like dead leaves, whirling in bands in the eddies. The cows and the horses struggled, tried to walk, and lost their footing. Our big gray horse fought long for life. He stretched his neck, he reared, snorting like a forge. But the enraged waters took him by the crupper, and we saw him, beaten, abandon himself.

Then we gave way for the first time. We felt the need of tears. Our hands stretched out to those dear animals that were being borne away, we lamented, giving vent to the tears and the sobs that we had suppressed. Ah! what ruin! The harvests destroyed, the cattle drowned, our fortunes changed in a few hours! God was not just! We had done nothing against Him, and He was taking everything from us! I shook my fist at the horizon. I spoke of our walk that afternoon, of our meadows, our wheat and vines that we had found so full of promise. It was all a lie, then! The sun lied when he sank, so sweet and calm, in the midst of the evening's serenity.

The water was still rising. Pierre, who was watching it, cried:

"Louis, we must look out! The water is up to the window!"

That warning snatched us from our spell of despair. I was once more myself. Shrugging my shoulders, I said:

"Money is nothing. As long as we are all saved, there need be no regrets. We shall have to work again—that is all!"

"Yes, yes; you are right, father," said Jacques, feverishly. "And we run no danger—the walls are good and strong. We must get up on the roof."

That was the only refuge left us. The water, which had mounted the stairs step by step, was already coming through the door. We rushed to the attic in a group, holding close to each other. Cyprien had disappeared. I called him, and I saw him return from the next room, his face working with emotion. Then, as I remarked the absence of the servants, for whom I was waiting, he gave me a strange look, then said, in a suppressed voice:

"Dead! The corner of the shed under their room caved in."

The poor girls must have gone to fetch their savings from their trunks. I told him to say nothing about it. A cold shiver had passed over me. It was Death entering the house.

When we went up, in our turn, we did not even think of putting out the lights. The cards remained spread upon the table. There was already a foot of water in the room.

## III.

Fortunately, the roof was vast and sloped gently. We reached it through a lid- like window, above which was a sort of platform. It was there that we took refuge. The women seated themselves. The men went over the tiles to reconnoiter. From my post against the dormer window through which we had climbed, I examined the four points of the horizon.

"Help cannot fail to arrive," I said, bravely. "The people of Saintin have boats; they will come this way. Look over there! Isn't that a lantern on the water?"

But no one answered me. Pierre had lighted his pipe, and he was smoking so furiously that, at each puff, he spit out pieces of the stem. Jacques and Cyprien looked into the distance, with drawn faces; while Gaspard, clenching his fists, continued to walk about, seeking an issue. At our feet the women, silent and shivering, hid their faces to shut out the sight. Yet Rose raised her head, glanced about her and demanded:

"And the servants? Where are they? Why, aren't they here?"

I avoided answering. She then questioned me, her eyes on mine.

"Where are the servants?"

I turned away, unable to lie. I felt that chill that had already brushed me pass over our women and our dear girls. They had understood. Marie burst into tears. Aimee wrapped her two children in her skirt, as if to protect them. Veronique, her face in her hands, did not move. Aunt Agathe, very pale, made the sign of the cross, and mumbled Paters and Aves.

Meanwhile the spectacle about us became of sovereign grandeur. The night retained the clearness of a summer night. There was no moon, but the sky was sprinkled with stars, and was of so pure a blue that it seemed to fill space with a blue light. And the immense sheet of water expanded beneath the softness of the sky. We could no longer see any land.

"The water is rising; the water is rising!" repeated my brother Pierre, still crunching the stem of his pipe between his teeth.

The water was within a yard of the roof. It was losing its tranquility; currents were being formed. In less than an hour the water became threatening, dashing against the house, bearing drifting barrels, pieces of wood, clumps of weeds. In the distance there were attacks upon walls, and we could hear the resounding shocks. Poplar trees fell, houses crumbled, like a cartload of stones emptied by the roadside.

Jacques, unnerved by the sobs of the women, cried:

"We can't stay here. We must try something. Father, I beg of you, try to do something."

I stammered after him:

"Yes, yes; let us try to do something."

And we knew of nothing. Gaspard offered to take Veronique on his back and swim with her to a place of safety. Pierre suggested a raft. Cyprien finally said:

"If we could only reach the church!"

Above the waters the church remained standing, with its little square steeple. We were separated from it by seven houses. Our farmhouse, the first of the village, adjoined a higher building, which, in turn, leaned against the next. Perhaps, by way of the roofs, we would be able to reach the parsonage. A number of people must have taken refuge there already, for the neighboring roofs were vacant, and we could hear voices that surely came from the steeple. But what dangers must be run to reach them!

"It is impossible," said Pierre. "The house of the Raimbeaus is too high; we would need ladders."

"I am going to try it," said Cyprien. "I will return if the way is impracticable. Otherwise, we will all go and we will have to carry the girls."

I let him go. He was right. We had to try the impossible. He had succeeded, by the aid of an iron hook fixed in a chimney, in climbing to the next house, when his wife, Aimee, raising her head, noticed that he was no longer with us. She screamed:

"Where is he? I don't want him to leave me! We are together, we shall die together!"

When she saw him on the top of the house she ran over the tiles, still holding her children. And she called out:

"Cyprien, wait for me! I am going with you. I am going to die with you."

She persisted. He leaned over, pleading with her, promising to come back, telling her that he was going for the rescue of all of us. But, with a wild air, she shook her head, repeating "I am going with you! I am going with you!"

He had to take the children. Then he helped her up. We could follow them along the crest of the house. They walked slowly. She had taken the children again, and at every step he turned and supported her.

"Get her to a safe place, and return!" I shouted.

I saw him wave his hand, but the roaring of the water prevented my hearing his answer. Soon we could not see them. They had descended to the roof of the next house. At the end of five minutes they appeared upon the third roof, which must have been very steep, for they went on hands and knees along the summit. A sudden terror seized me. I put my hands to my mouth and shouted:

"Come back! Come back!"

Then all of us shouted together. Our voices stopped them for a moment, but they continued on their way. They reached the angle formed by the street upon which faced the Raimbeau house, a high structure, with a roof at least ten feet above those of the neighboring houses. For a moment they hesitated. Then Cyprien climbed up a chimney pipe, with the agility of a cat. Aimee, who must have consented to wait for him, stood on the tiles. We saw her plainly, black and enlarged against the pale sky, straining her children to her bosom. And it was then that the horrifying trouble began.

The Raimbeau house, originally intended for a factory, was very flimsily built. Besides, the facade was exposed to the current in the street. I thought I could see it tremble from the attacks of the water; and, with a contraction of the throat, I watched Cyprien cross the roof. Suddenly a rumbling was heard. The moon rose, a round moon, whose yellow face lighted up the immense lake. Not a detail of the catastrophe was lost to us. The Raimbeau house collapsed. We gave a cry of terror as we saw Cyprien disappear. As the house crumbled we could distinguish nothing but a tempest, a swirling of waves beneath the debris of the roof. Then calm was restored, the surface became smooth; and out of the black hole of the engulfed house projected the skeleton of its framework. There was a mass of entangled beams, and, amongst them, I seemed to see a body moving, something living making superhuman efforts.

"He lives!" I cried. "Oh, God be praised! He lives!"

We laughed nervously; we clapped our hands, as if saved ourselves.

"He is going to raise himself up," said Pierre.

"Yes, yes," said Gaspard, "he is trying to seize the beam on his left."

But our laugh ceased. We had just realized the terrible situation in which Cyprien was placed. During the fall of the house his feet had been caught between two beams, and he hung head downward within a few inches of the water. On the roof of the next house Aimee was still standing, holding her two children. A convulsive tremor shook her. She did not take her eyes from her husband, a few yards below her. And, mad with horror, she emitted without cessation a lamentable sound like the howling of a dog.

"We can't let him die like that," said Jacques, distracted. "We must get down there."

"Perhaps we could slide down the beams and save him," remarked Pierre.

And they started toward the neighboring roof, when the second house collapsed, leaving a gap in the route. Then a chill seized us. We mechanically grasped each other's hands, wringing them cruelly as we watched the harrowing sight.

Cyprien had tried at first to stiffen his body. With extraordinary strength, he had lifted himself above the water, holding his body in an oblique position. Rut the strain was too great. Nevertheless, he struggled, tried to reach some of the beams, felt around him for something to hold to. Then, resigning himself, he fell back again, hanging limp.

Death was slow in coming. The water barely covered his hair, and it rose very gradually. He must have felt its coolness on his brain. A wave wet his brow; others closed his eyes. Slowly we saw his head disappear.

The women, at our feet, had buried their faces in their clasped hands. We, ourselves, fell to our knees, our arms outstretched, weeping, stammering supplications.

On the other roof Aimee, still standing, her children clasped to her bosom, howled mournfully into the night.

## IV.

I know not how long we remained in a stupor after that tragedy. When I came to, the water had risen. It was now on a level with the tiles. The roof was a narrow island, emerging from the immense sheet. To the right and the left the houses must have crumbled.

"We are moving," murmured Rose, who clung to the tiles.

And we all experienced the effect of rolling, as if the roof had become detached and turned into a raft. The swift currents seemed to be drifting us away. Then, when we looked at the church clock, immovable opposite us, the dizziness ceased; we found ourselves in the same place in the midst of the waves.

Then the water began an attack. Until then the stream had followed the street; but the debris that encumbered it deflected the course. And when a drifting object, a beam, came within reach of the current, it seized it and directed it against the house like a battering-ram. Soon ten, a dozen, beams were attacking us on all sides. The water roared. Our feet were spattered with foam. We heard the dull moaning of the house full of water. There were moments when the attacks became frenzied, when the beams battered fiercely; and then we thought that the end was near, that the walls would open and deliver us to the river.

Gaspard had risked himself upon the edge of the roof. He had seized a rafter and drawn it to him.

"We must defend ourselves," he cried.

Jacques, on his side, had stopped a long pole in its passage. Pierre helped him. I cursed my age that left me without strength, as feeble as a child. But the defense was organized—a drill between three men and a river. Gaspard, holding his beam in readiness, awaited the driftwood that the current sent against us, and be stopped it a short distance from the walls. At times the shock was so rude that he fell. Beside him Jacques and Pierre manipulated the long pole. During nearly an hour that unending fight continued. And the water retained its tranquil obstinacy, invincible.

Then Jacques and Pierre succumbed, prostrated; while Gaspard, in a last violent thrust, had his beam wrested from him by the current. The combat was useless.

Marie and Veronique had thrown themselves into each other's arms. They repeated incessantly one phrase—a phrase of terror that I still hear ringing in my ears:

"I don't want to die! I don't want to die!"

Rose put her arms about them. She tried to console them, to reassure them. And she herself, trembling, raised her face and cried out, in spite of herself:

"I don't want to die!"

Aunt Agathe alone said nothing. She no longer prayed, no longer made the sign of the cross. Bewildered, her eyes roamed about, and she tried to smile when her glance met mine.

The water was beating against the tiles now. There was no hope of help. We still heard the voices in the direction of the church; two lanterns had passed in the distance; and the silence spread over the immense yellow sheet. The people of Saintin, who owned boats, must have been surprised before us.

Gaspard continued to wander over the Roof. Suddenly he called us.

"Look!" he said. "Help me—hold me tight!"

He had a pole and be was watching an enormous black object that was gently drifting toward the house. It was the roof of a shed, made of strong boards, and that was floating like a raft. When it was within reach he stopped it with the pole, and, as he felt himself being carried off, he called to us. We held him around the waist.

Then, as the mass entered the current, it returned against our roof so violently that we were afraid of seeing it smashed into splinters.

Gaspard jumped upon it boldly. He went over it carefully, to assure himself of its solidity. He laughed, saying joyously:

"Grandfather, we are saved! Don't cry any more, you women. A real boat! Look, my feet are dry. And it will easily carry all of us!"

Still, he thought it well to make it more solid. He caught some floating beams and bound them to it with a rope that Pierre had brought up for an emergency. Gaspard even fell into the water, but at our screams he laughed. He knew the water well; he could swim three miles in the Garonne at a stretch. Getting up again, he shook himself, crying:

"Come, get on it! Don't lose any time!"

The women were on their knees. Gaspard had to carry Veronique and Marie to the middle of the raft, where he made them sit down.

Rose and Aunt Agathe slid down the tiles and placed themselves beside the young girls. At this moment I looked toward the church. Aimee was still in the same place. She was leaning now against a chimney, holding her children up at arm's length, for the water was to her waist.

"Don't grieve, grandfather," said Gaspard. "We will take her off on the way."

Pierre and Jacques were already on the raft, so I jumped on. Gaspard was the last one aboard. He gave us poles that he had prepared and that were to serve us as oars. He had a very long one that he used with great skill. We let him do all the commanding. At an order from him, we braced our poles against the tiles to put out into the stream. But it seemed as if the raft was attached to the roof. In spite of all our efforts, we could not budge it. At each new effort the current swung us violently against the house. And it was a dangerous manoeuvre, for the shock threatened to break up the planks composing the raft.

So once again we were made to feel our helplessness. We had thought ourselves saved, and we were still at the mercy of the river. I even regretted that the women were not on the roof; for, every minute, I expected to see them precipitated into the boiling torrent. But when I suggested regaining our refuge they all cried:

"No, no! Let us try again! Better die here!"

Gaspard no longer laughed. We renewed our efforts, bending to our poles with redoubled energy. Pierre then had the idea to climb up on the roof and draw us, by means of a rope, towards the left. He was thus able to draw us out of the current. Then, when he again jumped upon the raft, a few thrusts of our poles sent us out into the open. But Gaspard recalled the promise he had made me to stop for our poor Aimee, whose plaintive moans had never ceased. For that purpose it was necessary to cross the street, where the terrible current existed. He consulted me by a glance. I was completely upset. Never had such a combat raged within me. We would have to expose eight lives. And yet I had not the strength to resist the mournful appeal.

"Yes, yes," I said to Gaspard. "We can not possibly go away without her!"

He lowered his head without a word, and began using his pole against all the walls left standing. We passed the neighboring house, but as soon as we emerged into the street a cry escaped us. The current, which had again seized us, carried us back against our house. We were whirled round like a leaf, so rapidly that our cry was cut short by the smashing of the raft against the tiles. There was a rending sound, the planks were loosened and wrenched apart, and we were all thrown into the water. I do not know what happened then. I remember that when I sank I saw Aunt Agathe floating, sustained by her skirts, until she went down backward, head first, without a struggle.

A sharp pain brought me to. Pierre was dragging me by the hair along the tiles. I lay still, stupidly watching. Pierre had plunged in again. And, in my confused state, I was surprised to see Gaspard at the spot where my brother had disappeared. The young man had Veronique in his arms. When he had placed her near me he again jumped in, bringing up Marie, her face so waxy white that I thought her dead. Then he plunged again. But this time he searched in vain. Pierre had joined him. They talked and gave each other indications that I could not hear. As they drew themselves up on the roof, I cried:

"And Aunt Agathe? And Jacques? And Rose?"

They shook their heads. Large tears coursed down their cheeks. They explained to me that Jacques had struck his head against a beam and that Rose had been carried down with her husband's body, to which she clung. Aunt Agathe had not reappeared.

Raising myself, I looked toward the roof, where Aimee stood. The water was rising constantly. Aimee was now silent. I could see her upstretched arms holding her children out of the water. Then they all sank, the water closed over them beneath the drowsy light of the moon.

## V.

There were only five of us on the roof now. The water left us but a narrow band along the ridge. One of the chimneys had just been carried away. We had to raise Marie and Veronique, who were still unconscious, and support them almost in a standing position to prevent the waves washing over their legs. At last, their senses returned, and our anguish increased upon seeing them wet, shivering and crying miserably that they did not wish to die.

The end had come. The destroyed village was marked by a few vestiges of walls. Alone, the church reared its steeple intact, from whence came the voices—a murmur of human beings in a refuge. There were no longer any sounds of falling houses, like a cart of stones suddenly discharged. It was as if we were abandoned, shipwrecked, a thousand miles from land.

One moment we thought we heard the dip of oars. Ah! what hopeful music! How we all strained our eyes into space! We held our breath. But we could see nothing. The yellow sheet stretched away, spotted with black shadows. But none of those shadows—tops of trees, remnants of walls—moved. Driftwood, weeds, empty barrels caused us false joy. We waved our handkerchiefs until, realizing our error, we again succumbed to our anxiety.

"Ah, I see it!" cried Gaspard, suddenly. "Look over there. A large boat!"

And he pointed out a distant speck. I could see nothing, neither could Pierre. But Gaspard insisted it was a boat. The sound of oars became distinct. At last, we saw it. It was proceeding slowly and seemed to be circling about us without approaching. I remember that we were like mad. We raised our arms in our fury; we shouted with all our might. And we insulted the boat, called it cowardly. But, dark and silent, it glided away slowly. Was it really a boat? I do not know to this day. When it disappeared it carried our last hope.

We were expecting every second to be engulfed with the house. It was undermined and was probably supported by one solid wall, which, in giving way, would pull everything with it. But what terrified me most was to feel the roof sway under our feet. The house would perhaps hold out overnight, but the tiles were sinking in, beaten and pierced by beams. We had taken refuge on the left side on some solid rafters. Then these rafters seemed to weaken. Certainly they would sink if all five of us remained in so small a space.

For some minutes my brother Pierre had been twisting his soldierly mustache, frowning and muttering to himself. The growing danger that surrounded him and against which his courage availed nothing, was wearing out his endurance. He spat two or three times into the water, with an expression of contemptuous anger. Then, as we sank lower, he made up his mind; he started down the roof.

"Pierre! Pierre!" I cried, fearing to comprehend.

He turned and said quietly:

"Adieu, Louis! You see, it is too long for me. And it will leave more room for you."

And, first throwing in his pipe, he plunged, adding:

"Good night! I have had enough!"

He did not come up. He was not a strong swimmer, and he probably abandoned himself, heart-broken at the death of our dear ones and at our ruin.

Two o'clock sounded from the steeple of the church. The night would soon end— that horrible night already so filled with agony and tears. Little by little, beneath our feet, the small dry space grew smaller. The current had changed again. The drift, passed to the right of the village, floating slowly, as if the water, nearing its highest level, was reposing, tired and lazy.

Gaspard suddenly took off his shoes and his shirt. I watched him for a moment as he wrung his hands. When I questioned him he said:

"Listen, grandfather; it is killing me to wait. I cannot stay here. Let me do as I wish. I will save her."

He was speaking of Veronique. I opposed him. He would never have the strength to carry the young girl to the church. But he was obstinate.

"Yes, I can! My arms are strong. I feel myself able. You will see. I love her— I will save her!"

I was silent. I drew Marie to my breast. Then he thought I was reproaching the selfishness of his love. He stammered:

"I will return and get Marie. I swear it. I will find a boat and organize a rescue party. Have confidence in me, grandfather!"

Rapidly, he explained to Veronique that she must not struggle, that she must submit without a movement, and that she must not be afraid. The young girl answered "yes" to everything, with a distracted look. Then, after making the sign of the cross, he slid down the roof, holding Veronique by a rope that he had looped under her arms. She gave a scream, beat the water with arms and legs, and, suffocated, she fainted.

"I like this better!" Gaspard called to me. "Now, I can answer for her!"

It can be imagined with what agony I followed them with my eyes. On the white surface, I could see Gaspard's slightest movement. He held the young girl by means of the rope that he coiled around his neck; and he carried her thus, half thrown over his right shoulder. The crushing weight bore him under at times. But he advanced, swimming with superhuman strength. I was no longer in doubt. He had traversed a third of the distance when he struck against something submerged. The shock was terrible. Both disappeared. Then I saw him reappear alone. The rope must have snapped. He plunged twice. At last, he came up with Veronique, whom he again took on his back. But without the rope to hold her, she weighed him down more than ever. Still, he advanced. A tremor shook me as I saw them approaching the church. Suddenly, I saw some beams bearing down upon them. A second shock separated them and the waters closed over them.

From this moment, I was stupefied. I had but the instinct of the animal looking out for its own safety. When the water advanced, I retreated. In that stupor, I heard someone laughing, without explaining to myself who it was. The dawn appeared, a great white daybreak. It was very fresh and very calm, as on the bank of a pond, the surface of which awakens before sunrise. But the laughter sounded continually.

Turning, I saw Marie, standing in her wet clothes. It was she who was laughing.

Ah! the poor, dear child! How sweet and pretty she was at that early hour! I saw her stoop, take up some water in the hollow of her hand, and wash her face. Then she coiled her beautiful blonde hair. Doubtless, she imagined she was in her little room, dressing while the church bell rang merrily. And she continued to laugh her childish laugh, her eyes bright and her face happy.

I, too, began to laugh, infected with her madness. Terror had destroyed her mind; and it was a mercy, so charmed did she appear with the beauty of the morning.

I let her hasten, not understanding, shaking my head tenderly. When she considered herself ready to go, she sang one of her canticles in her clear crystalline voice. But, interrupting herself, she cried, as if responding to someone who had called her:

"I am coming, I am coming!"

She took up the canticle again, went down the roof, and entered the water. It covered her softly, without a ripple. I had not ceased smiling. I looked with happiness upon the spot where she had just disappeared.

Then, I remembered nothing more. I was alone on the roof. The water had risen. A chimney was standing, and I must have clung to it with all my strength, like an animal that dreads death. Then, nothing, nothing, a black pit, oblivion.

## VI.

Why am I still here? They tell me that people from Saintin came toward six o'clock, with boats, and that they found me lying on a chimney, unconscious. The water was cruel not to have carried me away to be with those who were dear to me.

All the others are gone! The babes in swaddling clothes, the girls to be married, the young married couples, the old married couples. And I, I live like a useless weed, coarse and dried, rooted in the rock. If I had the courage, I would say like Pierre:

"I have had enough! Good night!" And I would throw myself into the Garonne.

I have no child, my house is destroyed, my fields are devastated. Oh! the evenings when we were all at table, and the gaiety surrounded me and kept me young. Oh! the great days of harvest and vintage when we all worked, and when we returned to the house proud of our wealth! Oh! the handsome children and the fruitful vines, the beautiful girls and the golden grain, the joy of my old age, the living recompense of my entire life! Since all that is gone, why should I live?

There is no consolation. I do not want help. I will give my fields to the village people who still have their children. They will find the courage to clear the land of the flotsam and cultivate it anew. When one has no children, a corner is large enough to die in.

I had one desire, one only desire. I wished to recover the bodies of my family, to bury them beneath a slab, where I should soon rejoin them. It was said that, at Toulouse, a large number of bodies carried down the stream, had been taken from the water. I decided to make the trip.

What a terrible disaster! Nearly two thousand houses in ruins; seven hundred deaths; all the bridges carried away; a whole district razed, buried in the mud; atrocious tragedies; twenty thousand half-clad wretches starving to death; the city in a pestilential condition; mourning everywhere; the streets filled with funeral processions; financial aid powerless to heal the wounds! But I walked through it all without seeing anything. I had my ruins, I had my dead, to crush me.

I was told that many of the bodies had been buried in trenches in a corner of the cemetery. Only, they had had the forethought to photograph the unidentified. And it was among these lamentable photographs that I found Gaspard and Veronique. They had been clasped passionately in each other's arms, exchanging in death their bridal kiss. It had been necessary to break their arms in order to separate them. But, first, they had been photographed together; and they sleep together beneath the sod.

I have nothing but them, the image of those two handsome children; bloated by the water, disfigured, retaining upon their livid faces the heroism of their love. I look at them, and I weep.

# THE MILLER'S DAUGHTER

## CHAPTER I

### THE BETROTHAL

Pere Merlier's mill, one beautiful summer evening, was arranged for a grand fete. In the courtyard were three tables, placed end to end, which awaited the guests. Everyone knew that Francoise, Merlier's daughter, was that night to be betrothed to Dominique, a young man who was accused of idleness but whom the fair sex for three leagues around gazed at with sparkling eyes, such a fine appearance had he.

Pere Merlier's mill was pleasing to look upon. It stood exactly in the center of Rocreuse, where the highway made an elbow. The village had but one street, with two rows of huts, a row on each side of the road; but at the elbow meadows spread out, and huge trees which lined the banks of the Morelle covered the extremity of the valley with lordly shade. There was not, in all Lorraine, a corner of nature more adorable. To the right and to the left thick woods, centenarian forests, towered up from gentle slopes, filling the horizon with a sea of verdure, while toward the south the plain stretched away, of marvelous fertility, displaying as far as the eye could reach patches of ground divided by green hedges. But what constituted the special charm of Rocreuse was the coolness of that cut of verdure in the most sultry days of July and August. The Morelle descended from the forests of Gagny and seemed to have gathered the cold from the foliage beneath which it flowed for leagues; it brought with it the murmuring sounds, the icy and concentrated shade of the woods. And it was not the sole source of coolness: all sorts of flowing streams gurgled through the forest; at each step springs bubbled up; one felt, on following the narrow pathways, that there must exist subterranean lakes which pierced through beneath the moss and availed themselves of the smallest crevices at the feet of trees or between the rocks to burst forth in crystalline fountains. The whispering voices of these brooks were so numerous and so loud that they drowned the song of the bullfinches. It was like some enchanted park with cascades falling from every portion.

Below the meadows were damp. Gigantic chestnut trees cast dark shadows. On the borders of the meadows long hedges of poplars exhibited in lines their rustling branches. Two avenues of enormous plane trees stretched across the fields toward the ancient Chateau de Gagny, then a mass of ruins. In this constantly watered district the grass grew to an extraordinary height. It resembled a garden between two wooded hills, a natural garden, of which the meadows were the lawns, the giant trees marking the colossal flower beds. When the sun's rays at noon poured straight downward the shadows assumed a bluish tint; scorched grass slept in the heat, while an icy shiver passed beneath the foliage.

And there it was that Pere Merlier's mill enlivened with its ticktack a corner of wild verdure. The structure, built of plaster and planks, seemed as old as the world. It dipped partially in the Morelle, which rounded at that point into a transparent basin. A sluice had been made, and the water fell from a height of several meters upon the mill wheel, which cracked as it turned, with the asthmatic cough of a faithful servant grown old in the house. When Pere Merlier was advised to change it he shook his head, saying that a new wheel would be lazier and would not so well understand the work, and he mended the old one with whatever he could put his hands on: cask staves, rusty iron, zinc and lead. The wheel appeared gayer than ever for it, with its profile grown odd, all plumed with grass and moss. When the water beat upon it with its silvery flood it was covered with pearls; its strange carcass wore a sparkling attire of necklaces of mother-of-pearl.

The part of the mill which dipped in the Morelle had the air of a barbaric arch stranded there. A full half of the structure was built on piles. The water flowed beneath the floor, and deep places were there, renowned throughout the district for the enormous eels and crayfish caught in them. Below the fall the basin was as clear as a mirror, and when the wheel did not cover it with foam schools of huge fish could be seen swimming with the slowness of a squadron. Broken steps led down to the river near a stake to which a boat was moored. A wooden gallery passed above the wheel. Windows opened, pierced irregularly. It was a pell-mell of corners, of little walls, of constructions added too late, of beams and of roofs, which gave the mill the aspect of an old, dismantled citadel. But ivy had grown; all sorts of clinging plants stopped the too-wide chinks and threw a green cloak over the ancient building. The young ladies who passed by sketched Pere Merlier's mill in their albums.

On the side facing the highway the structure was more solid. A stone gateway opened upon the wide courtyard, which was bordered to the right and to the left by sheds and stables. Beside a well an immense elm covered half the courtyard with its shadow. In the background the building displayed the four windows of its second story, surmounted by a pigeon house. Pere Merlier's sole vanity was to have this front plastered every ten years. It had just received a new coating and dazzled the village when the sun shone on it at noon.

For twenty years Pere Merlier had been mayor of Rocreuse. He was esteemed for the fortune he had acquired. His wealth was estimated at something like eighty thousand francs, amassed sou by sou. When he married Madeleine Guillard, who brought him the mill as her dowry, he possessed only his two arms. But Madeleine never repented of her choice, so briskly did he manage the business. Now his wife was dead, and he remained a widower with his daughter Francoise. Certainly he might have rested, allowed the mill wheel to slumber in the moss, but that would have been too dull for him, and in his eyes the building would have seemed dead. He toiled on for pleasure.

Pere Merlier was a tall old man with a long, still face, who never laughed but who possessed, notwithstanding, a very gay heart. He had been chosen mayor because of his money and also on account of the imposing air he could assume during a marriage ceremony.

Francoise Merlier was just eighteen. She did not pass for one of the handsome girls of the district, as she was not robust. Up to her fifteenth year she had been even ugly.

The Rocreuse people had not been able to understand why the daughter of Pere and Mere Merlier, both of whom had always enjoyed excellent health, grew ill and with an air of regret. But at fifteen, though yet delicate, her little face became one of the prettiest in the world. She had black hair, black eyes, and was as rosy as a peach; her lips constantly wore a smile; there were dimples in her cheeks, and her fair forehead seemed crowned with sunlight. Although not considered robust in the district, she was far from thin; the idea was simply that she could not lift a sack of grain, but she would become plump as she grew older—she would eventually be as round and dainty as a quail. Her father's long periods of silence had made her thoughtful very young. If she smiled constantly it was to please others. By nature she was serious.

Of course all the young men of the district paid court to her, more on account of her ecus than her pretty ways. At last she made a choice which scandalized the community.

On the opposite bank of the Morelle lived a tall youth named Dominique Penquer. He did not belong to Rocreuse. Ten years before he had arrived from Belgium as the heir of his uncle, who had left him a small property upon the very border of the forest of Gagny, just opposite the mill, a few gunshots distant. He had come to sell this property, he said, and return home. But the district charmed him, it appeared, for he did not quit it. He was seen cultivating his little field, gathering a few vegetables upon which he subsisted. He fished and hunted; many times the forest guards nearly caught him and were on the point of drawing up proces-verbaux against him. This free existence, the resources of which the peasants could not clearly discover, at length gave him a bad reputation. He was vaguely styled a poacher. At any rate, he was lazy, for he was often found asleep on the grass when he should have been at work. The hut he inhabited beneath the last trees on the edge of the forest did not seem at all like the dwelling of an honest young fellow. If he had had dealings with the wolves of the ruins of Gagny the old women would not have been the least bit surprised. Nevertheless, the young girls sometimes risked defending him, for this doubtful man was superb; supple and tall as a poplar, he had a very white skin, with flaxen hair and beard which gleamed like gold in the sun.

One fine morning Francoise declared to Pere Merlier that she loved Dominique and would never wed any other man.

It may well be imagined what a blow this was to Pere Merlier. He said nothing, according to his custom, but his face grew thoughtful and his internal gaiety no longer sparkled in his eyes. He looked gruff for a week. Francoise also was exceedingly grave. What tormented Pere Merlier was to find out how this rogue of a poacher had managed to fascinate his daughter. Dominique had never visited the mill. The miller watched and saw the gallant on the other side of the

Morelle, stretched out upon the grass and feigning to be asleep. Francoise could see him from her chamber window. Everything was plain: they had fallen in love by casting sheep's eyes at each other over the mill wheel.

Another week went by. Francoise became more and more grave. Pere Merlier still said nothing. Then one evening he himself silently brought in Dominique. Francoise at that moment was setting the table. She did not seem astonished; she contented herself with putting on an additional plate, knife and fork, but the little dimples were again seen in her cheeks, and her smile reappeared. That morning Pere Merlier had sought out Dominique in his hut on the border of the wood.

There the two men had talked for three hours with doors and windows closed. What was the purport of their conversation no one ever knew. Certain it was, however, that Pere Merlier, on taking his departure, already called Dominique his son-in-law. Without doubt the old man had found the youth he had gone to seek a worthy youth in the lazy fellow who stretched himself out upon the grass to make the girls fall in love with him.

All Rocreuse clamored. The women at the doors had plenty to say on the subject of the folly of Pere Merlier, who had thus introduced a reprobate into his house. The miller let people talk on. Perhaps he remembered his own marriage. He was without a sou when he wedded Madeleine and her mill; this, however, had not prevented him from making a good husband. Besides, Dominique cut short the gossip by going so vigorously to work that all the district was amazed. The miller's assistant had just been drawn to serve as a soldier, and Dominique would not suffer another to be engaged. He carried the sacks, drove the cart, fought with the old mill wheel when it refused to turn, and all this with such good will that people came to see him out of curiosity. Pere Merlier had his silent laugh. He was excessively proud of having formed a correct estimate of this youth. There is nothing like love to give courage to young folks. Amid all these heavy labors Francoise and Dominique adored each other. They did not indulge in lovers' talks, but there was a smiling gentleness in their glances.

Up to that time Pere Merlier had not spoken a single word on the subject of marriage, and they respected this silence, awaiting the old man's will. Finally one day toward the middle of July he caused three tables to be placed in the courtyard, beneath the great elm, and invited his friends of Rocreuse to come in the evening and drink a glass of wine with him.

When the courtyard was full and all had their glasses in their hands, Pere Merlier raised his very high and said:

"I have the pleasure to announce to you that Francoise will wed this young fellow here in a month, on Saint Louis's Day."

Then they drank noisily. Everybody smiled. But Pere Merlier, again lifting his voice, exclaimed:

"Dominique, embrace your fiancee. It is your right."

They embraced, blushing to the tips of their ears, while all the guests laughed joyously. It was a genuine fete. They emptied a small cask of wine. Then when all were gone but intimate friends the conversation was carried on without noise. The night had fallen, a starry and cloudless night. Dominique and Francoise, seated side by side on a bench, said nothing.

An old peasant spoke of the war the emperor had declared against Prussia. All the village lads had already departed. On the preceding day troops had again passed through the place. There was going to be hard fighting.

"Bah!" said Pere Merlier with the selfishness of a happy man. "Dominique is a foreigner; he will not go to the war. And if the Prussians come here he will be on hand to defend his wife!"

The idea that the Prussians might come there seemed a good joke. They were going to receive a sound whipping, and the affair would soon be over.

"I have already seen them; I have already seen them," repeated the old peasant in a hollow voice.

There was silence. Then they drank again. Francoise and Dominique had heard nothing; they had gently taken each other by the hand behind the bench, so that nobody could see them, and it seemed so delightful that they remained where they were, their eyes plunged into the depths of the shadows.

What a warm and superb night it was! The village slumbered on both edges of the white highway in infantile quietude. From time to time was heard the crowing of some chanticleer aroused too soon. From the huge wood near by came long breaths, which passed over the roofs like caresses. The meadows, with their dark shadows, assumed a mysterious and dreamy majesty, while all the springs, all the flowing waters which gurgled in the darkness, seemed to be the cool and rhythmical respiration of the sleeping country. Occasionally the ancient mill wheel, lost in a doze, appeared to dream like those old watchdogs that bark while snoring; it cracked; it talked to itself, rocked by the fall of the Morelle, the surface of which gave forth the musical and continuous sound of an organ pipe. Never had more profound peace descended upon a happier corner of nature.

# CHAPTER II

## THE ATTACK ON THE MILL

A month later, on the day preceding that of Saint Louis, Rocreuse was in a state of terror. The Prussians had beaten the emperor and were advancing by forced marches toward the village. For a week past people who hurried along the highway had been announcing them thus: "They are at Lormiere—they are at Novelles!" And on hearing that they were drawing near so rapidly, Rocreuse every morning expected to see them descend from the wood of Gagny. They did not come, however, and that increased the fright. They would surely fall upon the village during the night and slaughter everybody.

That morning, a little before sunrise, there was an alarm. The inhabitants were awakened by the loud tramp of men on the highway. The women were already on their knees, making the sign of the cross, when some of the people, peering cautiously through the partially opened windows, recognized the red pantaloons. It was a French detachment. The captain immediately asked for the mayor of the district and remained at the mill after having talked with Pere Merlier.

The sun rose gaily that morning. It would be hot at noon. Over the wood floated a golden brightness, while in the distance white vapors arose from the meadows. The neat and pretty village awoke amid the fresh air, and the country, with its river and its springs, had the moist sweetness of a bouquet. But that beautiful day caused nobody to smile. The captain was seen to take a turn around the mill, examine the neighboring houses, pass to the other side of the Morelle and from there study the district with a field glass; Pere Merlier, who accompanied him, seemed to be giving him explanations. Then the captain posted soldiers behind the walls, behind the trees and in the ditches. The main body of the detachment encamped in the courtyard of the mill. Was there going to be a battle? When Pere Merlier returned he was questioned. He nodded his head without speaking. Yes, there was going to be a battle!

Francoise and Dominique were in the courtyard; they looked at him. At last he took his pipe from his mouth and said:

"Ah, my poor young ones, you cannot get married tomorrow!"

Dominique, his lips pressed together, with an angry frown on his forehead, at times raised himself on tiptoe and fixed his eyes upon the wood of Gagny, as if he wished to see the Prussians arrive. Francoise, very pale and serious, came and went, furnishing the soldiers with what they needed. The troops were making soup in a corner of the courtyard; they joked while waiting for it to get ready.

The captain was delighted. He had visited the chambers and the huge hall of the mill which looked out upon the river. Now, seated beside the well, he was conversing with Pere Merlier.

"Your mill is a real fortress," he said. "We can hold it without difficulty until evening. The bandits are late. They ought to be here."

The miller was grave. He saw his mill burning like a torch, but he uttered no complaint, thinking such a course useless. He merely said:

"You had better hide the boat behind the wheel; there is a place there just fit for that purpose. Perhaps it will be useful to have the boat."

The captain gave the requisite order. This officer was a handsome man of forty; he was tall and had an amiable countenance. The sight of Francoise and Dominique seemed to please him. He contemplated them as if he had forgotten the coming struggle. He followed Francoise with his eyes, and his look told plainly that he thought her charming. Then turning toward Dominique, he asked suddenly:

"Why are you not in the army, my good fellow?"

"I am a foreigner," answered the young man.

The captain evidently did not attach much weight to this reason. He winked his eye and smiled. Francoise was more agreeable company than a cannon. On seeing him smile, Dominique added:

"I am a foreigner, but I can put a ball in an apple at five hundred meters. There is my hunting gun behind you."

"You may have use for it," responded the captain dryly.

Francoise had approached, somewhat agitated. Without heeding the strangers present Dominique took and grasped in his the two hands she extended to him, as if to put herself under his protection. The captain smiled again but said not a word. He remained seated, his sword across his knees and his eyes plunged into space, lost in a reverie.

It was already ten o'clock. The heat had become very great. A heavy silence prevailed. In the courtyard, in the shadows of the sheds, the soldiers had begun to eat their soup. Not a sound came from the village; all its inhabitants had barricaded the doors and windows of their houses. A dog, alone upon the highway, howled. From the neighboring forests and meadows, swooning in the heat, came a prolonged and distant voice made up of all the scattered breaths. A cuckoo sang. Then the silence grew more intense.

Suddenly in that slumbering air a shot was heard. The captain leaped briskly to his feet; the soldiers left their plates of soup, yet half full. In a few seconds everybody was at the post of duty; from bottom to top the mill was occupied. Meanwhile the captain, who had gone out upon the road, had discovered nothing; to the right and to the left the highway stretched out, empty and white. A second shot was heard, and still nothing visible, not even a shadow. But as he was returning the captain perceived in the direction of Gagny, between two trees, a light puff of smoke whirling away like thistledown. The wood was calm and peaceful.

"The bandits have thrown themselves into the forest," he muttered. "They know we are here."

Then the firing continued, growing more and more vigorous, between the French soldiers posted around the mill and the Prussians hidden behind the trees. The balls whistled above the Morelle without damaging either side. The fusillade was irregular, the shots coming from every bush, and still only the little puffs of smoke, tossed gently by the breeze, were seen. This lasted nearly two hours. The officer hummed a tune with an air of indifference. Francoise and Dominique, who had remained in the courtyard, raised themselves on tiptoe and looked over a low wall. They were particularly interested in a little soldier posted on the shore of the Morelle, behind the remains of an old bateau; he stretched himself out flat on the ground, watched, fired and then glided into a ditch a trifle farther back to reload his gun; and his movements were so droll, so tricky and so supple, that they smiled as they looked at him. He must have perceived the head of a Prussian, for he arose quickly and brought his weapon to his shoulder, but before he could fire he uttered a cry, fell and rolled into the ditch, where for an instant his legs twitched convulsively like the claws of a chicken just killed. The little soldier had received a ball full in the breast. He was the first man slain. Instinctively Francoise seized Dominique's hand and clasped it with a nervous contraction.

"Move away," said the captain. "You are within range of the balls."

At that moment a sharp little thud was heard in the old elm, and a fragment of a branch came whirling down. But the two young folks did not stir; they were nailed to the spot by anxiety to see what was going on. On the edge of the wood a Prussian had suddenly come out from behind a tree as from a theater stage entrance, beating the air with his hands and falling backward. Nothing further moved; the two corpses seemed asleep in the broad sunlight; not a living soul was seen in the scorching country. Even the crack of the fusillade had ceased. The Morelle alone whispered in its clear tones.

Pere Merlier looked at the captain with an air of surprise, as if to ask him if the struggle was over.

"They are getting ready for something worse," muttered the officer. "Don't trust appearances. Move away from there."

He had not finished speaking when there was a terrible discharge of musketry. The great elm was riddled, and a host of leaves shot into the air. The Prussians had happily fired too high. Dominique dragged, almost carried, Francoise away, while Pere Merlier followed them, shouting:

"Go down into the cellar; the walls are solid!"

But they did not heed him; they entered the huge hall where ten soldiers were waiting in silence, watching through the chinks in the closed window shutters. The captain was alone in the courtyard, crouching behind the little wall, while the furious discharges continued. Without, the soldiers he had posted gave ground only foot by foot. However, they re-entered one by one, crawling, when the enemy had dislodged them from their hiding places. Their orders were to gain time and not show themselves, that the Prussians might remain in ignorance as to what force was before them. Another hour went by. As a sergeant arrived, saying that but two or three more men remained without, the captain glanced at his watch, muttering:

"Half-past two o'clock. We must hold the position four hours longer."

He caused the great gate of the courtyard to be closed, and every preparation was made for an energetic resistance. As the Prussians were on the opposite side of the Morelle, an immediate assault was not to be feared. There was a bridge two kilometers away, but they evidently were not aware of its existence, and it was hardly likely that they would attempt to ford the river. The officer, therefore, simply ordered the highway to be watched. Every effort would be made in the direction of the country.

Again the fusillade had ceased. The mill seemed dead beneath the glowing sun. Not a shutter was open; no sound came from the interior. At length, little by little, the Prussians showed themselves at the edge of the forest of Gagny. They stretched their necks and grew bold. In the mill several soldiers had already raised their guns to their shoulders, but the captain cried:

"No, no; wait. Let them come nearer."

They were exceedingly prudent, gazing at the mill with a suspicious air. The silent and somber old structure with its curtains of ivy filled them with uneasiness. Nevertheless, they advanced. When fifty of them were in the opposite meadow the officer uttered the single word:

"Fire!"

A crash was heard; isolated shots followed. Francoise, all of a tremble, had mechanically put her hands to her ears. Dominique, behind the soldiers, looked on; when the smoke had somewhat lifted he saw three Prussians stretched upon their backs in the center of the meadow. The others had thrown themselves behind the willows and poplars. Then the siege began.

For more than an hour the mill was riddled with balls. They dashed against the old walls like hail. When they struck the stones they were heard to flatten and fall into the water. They buried themselves in the wood with a hollow sound. Occasionally a sharp crack announced that the mill wheel had been hit. The soldiers in the interior were careful of their shots; they fired only when they could take aim. From time to time the captain consulted his watch. As a ball broke a shutter and plowed into the ceiling he said to himself:

"Four o'clock. We shall never be able to hold out!"

Little by little the terrible fusillade weakened the old mill. A shutter fell into the water, pierced like a bit of lace, and it was necessary to replace it with a mattress. Pere Merlier constantly exposed himself to ascertain the extent of the damage done to his poor wheel, the cracking of which made his heart ache. All would be over with it this time; never could he repair it. Dominique had implored Francoise to withdraw, but she refused to leave him; she was seated behind a huge oaken clothespress, which protected her. A ball, however, struck the clothespress, the sides of which gave forth a hollow sound. Then Dominique placed himself in front of Francoise. He had not yet fired a shot; he held his gun in his hand but was unable to approach the windows, which were altogether occupied by the soldiers. At each discharge the floor shook.

"Attention! Attention!" suddenly cried the captain.

He had just seen a great dark mass emerge from the wood. Immediately a formidable platoon fire opened. It was like a waterspout passing over the mill. Another shutter was shattered, and through the gaping opening of the window the balls entered. Two soldiers rolled upon the floor. One of them lay like a stone; they pushed the body against the wall because it was in the way. The other twisted in agony, begging his comrades to finish him, but they paid no attention to him. The balls entered in a constant stream; each man took care of himself and strove to find a loophole through which to return the fire. A third soldier was hit; he uttered not a word; he fell on the edge of a table, with eyes fixed and haggard. Opposite these dead men Francoise, stricken with horror, had mechanically pushed away her chair to sit on the floor against the wall; she thought she would take up less room there and not be in so much danger. Meanwhile the soldiers had collected all the mattresses of the household and partially stopped up the windows with them. The hall was filled with wrecks, with broken weapons and demolished furniture.

"Five o'clock," said the captain. "Keep up your courage! They are about to try to cross the river!"

At that moment Francoise uttered a cry. A ball which had ricocheted had grazed her forehead. Several drops of blood appeared. Dominique stared at her; then, approaching the window, he fired his first shot. Once started, he did not stop. He loaded and fired without heeding what was passing around him, but from time to time he glanced at Francoise. He was very deliberate and aimed with care. The Prussians, keeping beside the poplars, attempted the passage of the Morelle, as the captain had predicted, but as soon as a man strove to cross he fell, shot in the head by Dominique. The captain, who had his eyes on the young man, was amazed. He complimented him, saying that he should be glad to have many such skillful marksmen. Dominique did not hear him. A ball cut his shoulder; another wounded his arm, but he continued to fire.

There were two more dead men. The mangled mattresses no longer stopped the windows. The last discharge seemed as if it would have carried away the mill. The position had ceased to be tenable. Nevertheless, the captain said firmly:

"Hold your ground for half an hour more!"

Now he counted the minutes. He had promised his chiefs to hold the enemy in check there until evening, and he would not give an inch before the hour he had fixed on for the retreat. He preserved his amiable air and smiled upon Francoise to reassure her. He had picked up the gun of a dead soldier and himself was firing.

Only four soldiers remained in the hall. The Prussians appeared in a body on the other side of the Morelle, and it was clear that they intended speedily to cross the river. A few minutes more elapsed. The stubborn captain would not order the retreat. Just then a sergeant hastened to him and said:

"They are upon the highway; they will take us in the rear!"

The Prussians must have found the bridge. The captain pulled out his watch and looked at it.

"Five minutes longer," he said. "They cannot get here before that time!"

Then at six o'clock exactly he at last consented to lead his men out through a little door which opened into a lane. From there they threw themselves into a ditch; they gained the forest of Sauval. Before taking his departure the captain bowed very politely to Pere Merlier and made his excuses, adding:

"Amuse them! We will return!"

Dominique was now alone in the hall. He was still firing, hearing nothing, understanding nothing. He felt only the need of defending Francoise. He had not the least suspicion in the world that the soldiers had retreated. He aimed and killed his man at every shot. Suddenly there was a loud noise. The Prussians had entered the courtyard from behind. Dominique fired a last; shot, and they fell upon him while his gun was yet smoking.

Four men held him. Others vociferated around him in a frightful language. They were ready to slaughter him on the spot. Francoise, with a supplicating look, had cast herself before him. But an officer entered and ordered the prisoner to be delivered up to him. After exchanging a few words in German with the soldiers he turned toward Dominique and said to him roughly in very good French:

"You will be shot in two hours!"

## CHAPTER III

## THE FLIGHT

It was a settled rule of the German staff that every Frenchman, not belonging to the regular army, taken with arms in his hands should be shot. The militia companies themselves were not recognized as belligerents. By thus making terrible examples of the peasants who defended their homes, the Germans hoped to prevent the levy en masse, which they feared.

The officer, a tall, lean man of fifty, briefly questioned Dominique. Although he spoke remarkably pure French he had a stiffness altogether Prussian.

"Do you belong to this district?" he asked.

"No; I am a Belgian," answered the young man.

"Why then did you take up arms? The fighting did not concern you!"

Dominique made no reply. At that moment the officer saw Francoise who was standing by, very pale, listening; upon her white forehead her slight wound had put a red bar. He looked at the young folks, one after the other, seemed to understand matters and contented himself with adding:

"You do not deny having fired, do you?"

"I fired as often as I could!" responded Dominique tranquilly.

This confession was useless, for he was black with powder, covered with sweat and stained with a few drops of blood which had flowed from the scratch on his shoulder.

"Very well," said the officer. "You will be shot in two hours!"

Francoise did not cry out. She clasped her hands and raised them with a gesture of mute despair. The officer noticed this gesture. Two soldiers had taken Dominique to a neighboring apartment, where they were to keep watch over him. The young girl had fallen upon a chair, totally overcome; she could not weep; she was suffocating. The officer had continued to examine her. At last he spoke to her.

"Is that young man your brother?" he demanded.

She shook her head negatively. The German stood stiffly on his feet without a smile. Then after a short silence he again asked:

"Has he lived long in the district?"

She nodded affirmatively.

"In that case, he ought to be thoroughly acquainted with the neighboring forests."

This time she spoke.

"He is thoroughly acquainted with them, monsieur," she said, looking at him with considerable surprise.

He said nothing further to her but turned upon his heel, demanding that the mayor of the village should be brought to him. But Francoise had arisen with a slight blush on her countenance; thinking that she had seized the aim of the officer's questions, she had recovered hope. She herself ran to find her father.

Pere Merlier, as soon as the firing had ceased, had quickly descended to the wooden gallery to examine his wheel. He adored his daughter; he had a solid friendship for Dominique, his future son-in-law, but his wheel also held a large place in his heart. Since the two young ones, as he called them, had come safe and sound out of the fight, he thought of his other tenderness, which had suffered greatly. Bent over the huge wooden carcass, he was studying its wounds with a sad air. Five buckets were shattered to pieces; the central framework was riddled. He thrust his fingers in the bullet holes to measure their depth; he thought how he could repair all these injuries. Francoise found him already stopping up the clefts with rubbish and moss.

"Father," she said, "you are wanted."

And she wept at last as she told him what she had just heard. Pere Merlier tossed his head. People were not shot in such a summary fashion. The matter must be looked after. He re-entered the mill with his silent and tranquil air. When the officer demanded of him provisions for his men he replied that the inhabitants of Rocreuse were not accustomed to be treated roughly and that nothing would be obtained from them if violence were employed. He would see to everything but on condition that he was not interfered with. The officer at first seemed irritated by his calm tone; then he gave way before the old man's short and clear words. He even called him back and asked him:

"What is the name of that wood opposite?"

"The forest of Sauval."

"What is its extent?"

The miller looked at him fixedly.

"I do not know," he answered.

And he went away. An hour later the contribution of war in provisions and money, demanded by the officer, was in the courtyard of the mill. Night came on. Francoise watched with anxiety the movements of the soldiers. She hung about the room in which Dominique was imprisoned. Toward seven o'clock she experienced a poignant emotion. She saw the officer enter the prisoner's apartment and for a quarter of an hour heard their voices in loud conversation. For an instant the officer reappeared upon the threshold to give an order in German, which she did not understand, but when twelve men ranged themselves in the courtyard, their guns on their shoulders, she trembled and felt as if about to faint. All then was over: the execution was going to take place. The twelve men stood there ten minutes, Dominique's voice continuing to be raised in a tone of violent refusal. Finally the officer came out, saying, as he roughly shut the door:

"Very well; reflect. I give you until tomorrow morning."

And with a gesture he ordered the twelve men to break ranks. Francoise was stupefied. Pere Merlier, who had been smoking his pipe and looking at the platoon simply with an air of curiosity, took her by the arm with paternal gentleness. He led her to her chamber.

"Be calm," he said, "and try to sleep. Tomorrow, when it is light, we will see what can be done."

As he withdrew he prudently locked her in. It was his opinion that women were good for nothing and that they spoiled everything when they took a hand in a serious affair. But Francoise did not retire. She sat for a long while upon the side of her bed, listening to the noises of the house. The German soldiers encamped in the courtyard sang and laughed; they must have been eating and drinking until eleven o'clock, for the racket did not cease an instant. In the mill itself heavy footsteps resounded from time to time, without doubt those of the sentinels who were being relieved. But she was interested most by the sounds she could distinguish in the apartment beneath her chamber. Many times she stretched herself out at full length and put her ear to the floor. That apartment was the one in which Dominique was confined. He must have been walking back and forth from the window to the wall, for she long heard the regular cadence of his steps. Then deep silence ensued; he had doubtless seated himself. Finally every noise ceased and all was as if asleep. When slumber appeared to her to have settled on the house she opened her window as gently as possible and leaned her elbows on the sill.

Without, the night had a warm serenity. The slender crescent of the moon, which was sinking behind the forest of Sauval, lit up the country with the glimmer of a night lamp. The lengthened shadows of the tall trees barred the meadows with black, while the grass in uncovered spots assumed the softness of greenish velvet. But Francoise did not pause to admire the mysterious charms of the night. She examined the country, searching for the sentinels whom the Germans had posted obliquely. She clearly saw their shadows extending like the rounds of a ladder along the Morelle. Only one was before the mill, on the other shore of the river, beside a willow, the branches of which dipped in the water. Francoise saw him plainly. He was a tall man and was standing motionless, his face turned toward the sky with the dreamy air of a shepherd.

When she had carefully inspected the locality she again seated herself on her bed. She remained there an hour, deeply absorbed. Then she listened once more: there was not a sound in the mill. She returned to the window and glanced out, but doubtless one of the horns of the moon, which was still visible behind the trees, made her uneasy, for she resumed her waiting attitude. At last she thought the proper time had come. The night was as black as jet; she could no longer see the sentinel opposite; the country spread out like a pool of ink. She strained her ear for an instant and made her decision. Passing near the window was an iron ladder, the bars fastened to the wall, which mounted from the wheel to the garret and formerly enabled the millers to reach certain machinery; afterward the mechanism had been altered, and for a long while the ladder had been hidden under the thick ivy which covered that side of the mill.

Francoise bravely climbed out of her window and grasped one of the bars of the ladder. She began to descend. Her skirts embarrassed her greatly. Suddenly a stone was detached from the wall and fell into the Morelle with a loud splash. She stopped with an icy shiver of fear. Then she realized that the waterfall with its continuous roar would drown every noise she might make, and she descended more courageously, feeling the ivy with her foot, assuring herself that the rounds were firm. When she was at the height of the chamber which served as Dominique's prison she paused. An unforeseen difficulty nearly caused her to lose all her courage: the window of the chamber was not directly below that of her apartment. She hung off from the ladder, but when she stretched out her arm her hand encountered only the wall. Must she, then, ascend without pushing her plan to completion? Her arms were fatigued; the murmur of the Morelle beneath her commenced to make her dizzy. Then she tore from the wall little fragments of plaster and threw them against Dominique's window. He did not hear; he was doubtless asleep. She crumbled more plaster from the wall, scraping the skin off her fingers. She was utterly exhausted; she felt herself falling backward, when Dominique at last softly opened the window.

"It is I!" she murmured. "Catch me quickly; I'm falling!"

It was the first time that she had addressed him familiarly. Leaning out, he seized her and drew her into the chamber. There she gave vent to a flood of tears, stifling her sobs that she might not be heard. Then by a supreme effort she calmed herself.

"Are you guarded?" she asked in a low voice.

Dominique, still stupefied at seeing her thus, nodded his head affirmatively, pointing to the door. On the other side they heard someone snoring; the sentinel, yielding to sleep, had thrown himself on the floor against the door, arguing that by disposing himself thus the prisoner could not escape.

"You must fly," resumed Francoise excitedly. "I have come to beg you to do so and to bid you farewell."

But he did not seem to hear her. He repeated:

"What? Is it you; is it you? Oh, what fear you caused me! You might have killed yourself!"

He seized her hands; he kissed them.

"How I love you, Francoise!" he murmured. "You are as courageous as good. I had only one dread: that I should die without seeing you again. But you are here, and now they can shoot me. When I have passed a quarter of an hour with you I shall be ready."

Little by little he had drawn her to him, and she leaned her head upon his shoulder. The danger made them dearer to each other. They forgot everything in that warm clasp.

"Ah, Francoise," resumed Dominique in a caressing voice, "this is Saint Louis's Day, the day, so long awaited, of our marriage. Nothing has been able to separate us, since we are both here alone, faithful to the appointment. Is not this our wedding morning?"

"Yes, yes," she repeated, "it is our wedding morning."

They tremblingly exchanged a kiss. But all at once she disengaged herself from Dominique's arms; she remembered the terrible reality.

"You must fly; you must fly," she whispered. "There is not a minute to be lost!"

And as he stretched out his arms in the darkness to clasp her again, she said tenderly:

"Oh, I implore you to listen to me! If you die I shall die also! In an hour it will be light. I want you to go at once."

Then rapidly she explained her plan. The iron ladder descended to the mill wheel; there he could climb down the buckets and get into the boat which was hidden away in a nook. Afterward it would be easy for him to reach the other bank of the river and escape.

"But what of the sentinels?" he asked.

"There is only one, opposite, at the foot of the first willow."

"What if he should see me and attempt to give an alarm?"

Francoise shivered. She placed in his hand a knife she had brought with her. There was a brief silence.

"What is to become of your father and yourself?" resumed Dominique. "No, I cannot fly! When I am gone those soldiers will, perhaps, massacre you both! You do not know them. They offered me my life if I would consent to guide them through the forest of Sauval. When they discover my escape they will be capable of anything!"

The young girl did not stop to argue. She said simply in reply to all the reasons he advanced:

"Out of love for me, fly! If you love me, Dominique, do not remain here another moment!"

Then she promised to climb back to her chamber. No one would know that she had helped him. She finally threw her arms around him to convince him with an embrace, with a burst of extraordinary love. He was vanquished. He asked but one more question:

"Can you swear to me that your father knows what you have done and that he advises me to fly?"

"My father sent me!" answered Francoise boldly.

She told a falsehood. At that moment she had only one immense need: to know that he was safe, to escape from the abominable thought that the sun would be the signal for his death. When he was far away every misfortune might fall upon her; that would seem delightful to her from the moment he was secure. The selfishness of her tenderness desired that he should live before everything.

"Very well," said Dominique; "I will do what you wish."

They said nothing more. Dominique reopened the window. But suddenly a sound froze them. The door was shaken, and they thought that it was about to be opened. Evidently a patrol had heard their voices. Standing locked in each other's arms, they waited in unspeakable anguish. The door was shaken a second time, but it did not open. They uttered low sighs of relief; they comprehended that the soldier who was asleep against the door must have turned over. In fact, silence succeeded; the snoring was resumed.

Dominique exacted that Francoise should ascend to her chamber before he departed. He clasped her in his arms and bade her a mute adieu. Then he aided her to seize the ladder and clung to it in his turn. But he refused to descend a single round until convinced that she was in her apartment. When Francoise had entered her window she let fall in a voice as light as a breath:

"Au revoir, my love!"

She leaned her elbows on the sill and strove to follow Dominique with her eyes. The night was yet very dark. She searched for the sentinel but could not see him; the willow alone made a pale stain in the midst of the gloom. For an instant she heard the sound produced by Dominique's body in passing along the ivy. Then the wheel cracked, and there was a slight agitation in the water which told her that the young man had found the boat. A moment afterward she distinguished the somber silhouette of the bateau on the gray surface of the Morelle. Terrible anguish seized upon her. Each instant she thought she heard the sentinel's cry of alarm; the smallest sounds scattered through the gloom seemed to her the hurried tread of soldiers, the clatter of weapons, the charging of guns. Nevertheless, the seconds elapsed and the country maintained its profound peace. Dominique must have reached the other side of the river. Francoise saw nothing more. The silence was majestic. She heard a shuffling of feet, a hoarse cry and the hollow fall of a body. Afterward the silence grew deeper. Then as if she had felt Death pass by, she stood, chilled through and through, staring into the thick night.

# CHAPTER IV

## A TERRIBLE EXPERIENCE

At dawn a clamor of voices shook the mill. Pere Merlier opened the door of Francoise's chamber. She went down into the courtyard, pale and very calm. But there she could not repress a shiver as she saw the corpse of a Prussian soldier stretched out on a cloak beside the well.

Around the body troops gesticulated, uttering cries of fury. Many of them shook their fists at the village. Meanwhile the officer had summoned Pere Merlier as the mayor of the commune.

"Look!" he said to him in a voice almost choking with anger. "There lies one of our men who was found assassinated upon the bank of the river. We must make a terrible example, and I count on you to aid us in discovering the murderer."

"As you choose," answered the miller with his usual stoicism, "but you will find it no easy task."

The officer stooped and drew aside a part of the cloak which hid the face of the dead man. Then appeared a horrible wound. The sentinel had been struck in the throat, and the weapon had remained in the cut. It was a kitchen knife with a black handle.

"Examine that knife," said the officer to Pere Merlier; "perhaps it will help us in our search."

The old man gave a start but recovered control of himself immediately. He replied without moving a muscle of his face:

"Everybody in the district has similar knives. Doubtless your man was weary of fighting and put an end to his own life. It looks like it!"

"Mind what you say!" cried the officer furiously. "I do not know what prevents me from setting fire to the four corners of the village!"

Happily in his rage he did not notice the deep trouble pictured on Francoise's countenance. She had been forced to sit down on a stone bench near the well. Despite herself her eyes were fixed upon the corpse stretched our on the ground almost at her feet. It was that of a tall and handsome man who resembled Dominique, with flaxen hair and blue eyes. This resemblance made her heart ache. She thought that perhaps the dead soldier had left behind him in Germany a sweetheart who would weep her eyes out for him. She recognized her knife in the throat of the murdered man. She had killed him.

The officer was talking of striking Rocreuse with terrible measures, when soldiers came running to him. Dominique's escape had just been discovered. It caused an extreme agitation. The officer went to the apartment in which the prisoner had been confined, looked out of the window which had remained open, understood everything and returned, exasperated.

Pere Merlier seemed greatly vexed by Dominique's flight.

"The imbecile!" he muttered. "He has ruined all!"

Francoise heard him and was overcome with anguish. But the miller did not suspect her of complicity in the affair. He tossed his head, saying to her in an undertone:

"We are in a nice scrape!"

"It was that wretch who assassinated the soldier! I am sure of it!" cried the officer. "He has undoubtedly reached the forest. But he must be found for us or the village shall pay for him!"

Turning to the miller, he said:

"See here, you ought to know where he is hidden!"

Pere Merlier laughed silently, pointing to the wide stretch of wooden hills.

"Do you expect to find a man in there?" he said.

"Oh, there must be nooks there with which you are acquainted. I will give you ten men. You must guide them."

"As you please. But it will take a week to search all the wood in the vicinity."

The old man's tranquillity enraged the officer. In fact, the latter comprehended the absurdity of this search. At that moment he saw Francoise, pale and trembling, on the bench. The anxious attitude of the young girl struck him. He was silent for an instant, during which he in turn examined the miller and his daughter.

At length he demanded roughly of the old man:

"Is not that fellow your child's lover?"

Pere Merlier grew livid and seemed about to hurl himself upon the officer to strangle him. He stiffened himself but made no answer. Francoise buried her face in her hands.

"Yes, that's it!" continued the Prussian. "And you or your daughter helped him to escape! One of you is his accomplice! For the last time, will you give him up to us?"

The miller uttered not a word. He turned away and looked into space with an air of indifference, as if the officer had not addressed him. This brought the latter's rage to a head.

"Very well!" he shouted. "You shall be shot in his place!"

And he again ordered out the platoon of execution. Pere Merlier remained as stoical as ever. He hardly even shrugged his shoulders; all this drama appeared to him in bad taste. Without doubt he did not believe that they would shoot a man so lightly. But when the platoon drew up before him he said gravely:

"So it is serious, is it? Go on with your bloody work then! If you must have a victim I will do as well as another!"

But Francoise started up, terrified, stammering:

"In pity, monsieur, do no harm to my father! Kill me in his stead! I aided Dominique to fly! I alone am guilty!"

"Hush, my child!" cried Pere Merlier. "Why do you tell an untruth? She passed the night locked in her chamber, monsieur. She tells a falsehood, I assure you!"

"No, I do not tell a falsehood!" resumed the young girl ardently. "I climbed out of my window and went down the iron ladder; I urged Dominique to fly. This is the truth, the whole truth!"

The old man became very pale. He saw clearly in her eyes that she did not lie, and her story terrified him. Ah, these children with their hearts, how they spoil everything! Then he grew angry and exclaimed:

"She is mad; do not heed her. She tells you stupid tales. Come, finish your work!"

She still protested. She knelt, clasping her hands. The officer tranquilly watched this dolorous struggle.

"MON DIEU!" he said at last. "I take your father because I have not the other. Find the fugitive and the old man shall be set at liberty!"

She gazed at him with staring eyes, astonished at the atrocity of the proposition.

"How horrible!" she murmured. "Where do you think I can find Dominique at this hour? He has departed; I know no more about him."

"Come, make your choice—him or your father."

"Oh, MON DIEU! How can I choose? If I knew where Dominique was I could not choose! You are cutting my heart. I would rather die at once. Yes, it would be the sooner over. Kill me, I implore you, kill me!"

This scene of despair and tears finally made the officer impatient. He cried out:

"Enough! I will be merciful. I consent to give you two hours. If in that time your lover is not here your father will be shot in his place!"

He caused Pere Merlier to be taken to the chamber which had served as Dominique's prison. The old man demanded tobacco and began to smoke. Upon his impassible face not the slightest emotion was visible. But when alone, as he smoked, he shed two big tears which ran slowly down his cheeks. His poor, dear child, how she was suffering!

Francoise remained in the middle of the courtyard. Prussian soldiers passed, laughing. Some of them spoke to her, uttered jokes she could not understand. She stared at the door through which her father had disappeared. With a slow movement she put her hand to her forehead, as if to prevent it from bursting.

The officer turned upon his heel, saying:

"You have two hours. Try to utilize them."

She had two hours. This phrase buzzed in her ears. Then mechanically she quitted the courtyard; she walked straight ahead. Where should she go?—what should she do? She did not even try to make a decision because she well understood the inutility of her efforts. However, she wished to see Dominique. They could have an understanding together; they might, perhaps, find an expedient. And amid the confusion of her thoughts she went down to the shore of the Morelle, which she crossed below the sluice at a spot where there were huge stones. Her feet led her beneath the first willow, in the corner of the meadow. As she stooped she saw a pool of blood which made her turn pale. It was there the murder had been committed. She followed the track of

Dominique in the trodden grass; he must have run, for she perceived a line of long footprints stretching across the meadow. Then farther on she lost these traces. But in a neighboring field she thought she found them again. The new trail conducted her to the edge of the forest, where every indication was effaced.

Francoise, nevertheless, plunged beneath the trees. It solaced her to be alone. She sat down for an instant, but at the thought that time was passing she leaped to her feet. How long had it been since she left the mill? Five minutes?—half an hour? She had lost all conception of time. Perhaps Dominique had concealed himself in a copse she knew of, where they had one afternoon eaten filberts together. She hastened to the copse, searched it. Only a blackbird flew away, uttering its soft, sad note. Then she thought he might have taken refuge in a hollow of the rocks, where it had sometimes been his custom to lie in wait for game, but the hollow of the rocks was empty. What good was it to hunt for him? She would never find him, but little by little the desire to discover him took entire possession of her, and she hastened her steps. The idea that he might have climbed a tree suddenly occurred to her. She advanced with uplifted eyes, and that he might be made aware of her presence she called him every fifteen or twenty steps. Cuckoos answered; a breath of wind which passed through the branches made her believe that he was there and was descending. Once she even imagined she saw him; she stopped, almost choked, and wished to fly. What was she to say to him? Had she come to take him back to be shot? Oh no, she would not tell him what had happened. She would cry out to him to escape, not to remain in the neighborhood. Then the thought that her father was waiting for her gave her a sharp pain. She fell upon the turf, weeping, crying aloud:

"MON DIEU! MON DIEU! Why am I here?"

She was mad to have come. And as if seized with fear, she ran; she sought to leave the forest. Three times she deceived herself; she thought she never again would find the mill, when she entered a meadow just opposite Rocreuse. As soon as she saw the village she paused. Was she going to return alone? She was still hesitating when a voice softly called:

"Francoise! Francoise!"

And she saw Dominique, who had raised his head above the edge of a ditch. Just God! She had found him! Did heaven wish his death? She restrained a cry; she let herself glide into the ditch.

"Are you searching for me?" asked the young man.

"Yes," she answered, her brain in a whirl, not knowing what she said.

"What has happened?"

She lowered her eyes, stammered:

"Nothing. I was uneasy; I wanted to see you."

Then, reassured, he explained to her that he had resolved not to go away. He was doubtful about the safety of herself and her father. Those Prussian wretches were fully capable of taking vengeance upon women and old men. But everything was getting on well. He added with a laugh:

"Our wedding will take place in a week—I am sure of it."

Then as she remained overwhelmed, he grew grave again and said:

"But what ails you? You are concealing something from me!"

"No; I swear it to you. I am out of breath from running."

He embraced her, saying that it was imprudent for them to be talking, and he wished to climb out of the ditch to return to the forest. She restrained him. She trembled.

"Listen," she said: "it would, perhaps, be wise for you to remain where you are. No one is searching for you; you have nothing to fear."

"Francoise, you are concealing something from me," he repeated.

Again she swore that she was hiding nothing. She had simply wished to know that he was near her. And she stammered forth still further reasons. She seemed so strange to him that he now could not be induced to flee. Besides, he had faith in the return of the French. Troops had been seen in the direction of Sauval.

"Ah, let them hurry; let them get here as soon as possible," she murmured fervently.

At that moment eleven o'clock sounded from the belfry of Rocreuse. The strokes were clear and distinct. She arose with a terrified look; two hours had passed since she quitted the mill.

"Hear me," she said rapidly: "if we have need of you I will wave my handkerchief from my chamber window."

And she departed on a run, while Dominique, very uneasy, stretched himself out upon the edge of the ditch to watch the mill. As she was about to enter Rocreuse, Francoise met an old beggar, Pere Bontemps, who knew everybody in the district. He bowed to her; he had just seen the miller in the midst of the Prussians; then, making the sign of the cross and muttering broken words, he went on his way.

"The two hours have passed," said the officer when Francoise appeared.

Pere Merlier was there, seated upon the bench beside the well. He was smoking. The young girl again begged, wept, sank on her knees. She wished to gain time. The hope of seeing the French return had increased in her, and while lamenting she thought she heard in the distance, the measured tramp of an army. Oh, if they would come, if they would deliver them all?

"Listen, monsieur," she said: "an hour, another hour; you can grant us another hour!"

But the officer remained inflexible. He even ordered two men to seize her and take her away, that they might quietly proceed with the execution of the old man. Then a frightful struggle took place in Francoise's heart. She could not allow her father to be thus assassinated. No, no; she would die rather with Dominique. She was running toward her chamber when Dominique himself entered the courtyard.

The officer and the soldiers uttered a shout of triumph. But the young man, calmly, with a somewhat severe look, went up to Francoise, as if she had been the only person present.

"You did wrong," he said. "Why did you not bring me back? It remained for Pere Bontemps to tell me everything. But I am here!"

## CHAPTER V

## THE RETURN OF THE FRENCH

It was three o'clock in the afternoon. Great black clouds, the trail of some neighboring storm, had slowly filled the sky. The yellow heavens, the brass covered uniforms, had changed the valley of Rocreuse, so gay in the sunlight, into a den of cutthroats full of sinister gloom. The Prussian officer had contented himself with causing Dominique to be imprisoned without announcing what fate he reserved for him. Since noon Francoise had been torn by terrible anguish. Despite her father's entreaties she would not quit the courtyard. She was awaiting the French. But the hours sped on; night was approaching, and she suffered the more as all the time gained did not seem to be likely to change the frightful denouement.

About three o'clock the Prussians made their preparations for departure. For an instant past the officer had, as on the previous day, shut himself up with Dominique. Francoise realized that the young man's life was in balance. She clasped her hands; she prayed. Pere Merlier, beside her, maintained silence and the rigid attitude of an old peasant who does not struggle against fate.

"Oh, MON DIEU! Oh, MON DIEU!" murmured Francoise. "They are going to kill him!"

The miller drew her to him and took her on his knees as if she had been a child.

At that moment the officer came out, while behind him two men brought Dominique.

"Never! Never!" cried the latter. "I am ready to die!"

"Think well," resumed the officer. "The service you refuse me another will render us. I am generous: I offer you your life. I want you simply to guide us through the forest to Montredon. There must be pathways leading there."

Dominique was silent.

"So you persist in your infatuation, do you?"

"Kill me and end all this!" replied the young man.

Francoise, her hands clasped, supplicated him from afar. She had forgotten everything; she would have advised him to commit an act of cowardice. But Pere Merlier seized her hands that the Prussians might not see her wild gestures.

"He is right," he whispered: "it is better to die!"

The platoon of execution was there. The officer awaited a sign of weakness on Dominique's part. He still expected to conquer him. No one spoke. In the distance violent crashes of thunder were heard. Oppressive heat weighed upon the country. But suddenly, amid the silence, a cry broke forth:

"The French! The French!"

Yes, the French were at hand. Upon the Sauval highway, at the edge of the wood, the line of red pantaloons could be distinguished. In the mill there was an extraordinary agitation. The Prussian soldiers ran hither and thither with guttural exclamations. Not a shot had yet been fired.

"The French! The French!" cried Francoise, clapping her hands.

She was wild with joy. She escaped from her father's grasp; she laughed and tossed her arms in the air. At last they had come and come in time, since Dominique was still alive!

A terrible platoon fire, which burst upon her ears like a clap of thunder, caused her to turn. The officer muttered between his teeth:

"Before everything, let us settle this affair!"

And with his own hand pushing Dominique against the wall of a shed he ordered his men to fire. When Francoise looked Dominique lay upon the ground with blood streaming from his neck and shoulders.

She did not weep; she stood stupefied. Her eyes grew fixed, and she sat down under the shed, a few paces from the body. She stared at it, wringing her hands. The Prussians had seized Pere Merlier as a hostage.

It was a stirring combat. The officer had rapidly posted his men, comprehending that he could not beat a retreat without being cut to pieces. Hence he would fight to the last. Now the Prussians defended the mill, and the French attacked it. The fusillade began with unusual violence. For half an hour it did not cease. Then a hollow sound was heard, and a ball broke a main branch of the old elm. The French had cannon. A battery, stationed just above the ditch in which Dominique had hidden himself, swept the wide street of Rocreuse. The struggle could not last long.

Ah, the poor mill! Balls pierced it in every part. Half of the roof was carried away. Two walls were battered down. But it was on the side of the Morelle that the destruction was most lamentable. The ivy, torn from the tottering edifice, hung like rags; the river was encumbered with wrecks of all kinds, and through a breach was visible Francoise's chamber with its bed, the white curtains of which were carefully closed. Shot followed shot; the old wheel received two balls and gave vent to an agonizing groan; the buckets were borne off by the current; the framework was crushed. The soul of the gay mill had left it!

Then the French began the assault. There was a furious fight with swords and bayonets. Beneath the rust-colored sky the valley was choked with the dead. The broad meadows had a wild look with their tall, isolated trees and their hedges of poplars which stained them with shade. To the right and to the left the forests were like the walls of an ancient amphitheater which enclosed the fighting gladiators, while the springs, the fountains and the flowing brooks seemed to sob amid the panic of the country.

Beneath the shed Francoise still sat near Dominique's body; she had not moved. Pere Merlier had received a slight wound. The Prussians were exterminated, but the ruined mill was on fire in a dozen places. The French rushed into the courtyard, headed by their captain. It was his first success of the war. His face beamed with triumph. He waved his sword, shouting:

"Victory! Victory!"

On seeing the wounded miller, who was endeavoring to comfort Francoise, and noticing the body of Dominique, his joyous look changed to one of sadness.

Then he knelt beside the young man and, tearing open his blouse, put his hand to his heart.

"Thank God!" he cried. "It is yet beating! Send for the surgeon!"

At the captain's words Francoise leaped to her feet.

"There is hope!" she cried. "Oh, tell me there is hope!"

At that moment the surgeon appeared. He made a hasty examination and said:

"The young man is severely hurt, but life is not extinct; he can be saved!" By the surgeon's orders Dominique was transported to a neighboring cottage, where he was placed in bed. His wounds were dressed; restoratives were administered, and he soon recovered consciousness. When he opened his eyes he saw Francoise sitting beside him and through the open window caught sight of Pere Merlier talking with the French captain. He passed his hand over his forehead with a bewildered air and said:

"They did not kill me after all!"

"No," replied Francoise. "The French came, and their surgeon saved you."

Pere Merlier turned and said through the window:

"No talking yet, my young ones!"

In due time Dominique was entirely restored, and when peace again blessed the land he wedded his beloved Francoise.

The mill was rebuilt, and Pere Merlier had a new wheel upon which to bestow whatever tenderness was not engrossed by his daughter and her husband.

# CAPTAIN BURLE

## CHAPTER I

THE SWINDLE

It was nine o'clock. The little town of Vauchamp, dark and silent, had just retired to bed amid a chilly November rain. In the Rue des Recollets, one of the narrowest and most deserted streets of the district of Saint-Jean, a single window was still alight on the third floor of an old house, from whose damaged gutters torrents of water were falling into the street. Mme Burle was sitting up before a meager fire of vine stocks, while her little grandson Charles pored over his lessons by the pale light of a lamp.

The apartment, rented at one hundred and sixty francs per annum, consisted of four large rooms which it was absolutely impossible to keep warm during the winter. Mme Burle slept in the largest chamber, her son Captain and Quartermaster Burle occupying a somewhat smaller one overlooking the street, while little Charles had his iron cot at the farther end of a spacious drawing room with mildewed hangings, which was never used. The few pieces of furniture belonging to the captain and his mother, furniture of the massive style of the First Empire, dented and worn by continuous transit from one garrison town to another, almost disappeared from view beneath the lofty ceilings whence darkness fell. The flooring of red-colored tiles was cold and hard to the feet; before the chairs there were merely a few threadbare little rugs of poverty-stricken aspect, and athwart this desert all the winds of heaven blew through the disjointed doors and windows.

Near the fireplace sat Mme Burle, leaning back in her old yellow velvet armchair and watching the last vine branch smoke, with that stolid, blank stare of the aged who live within themselves. She would sit thus for whole days together, with her tall figure, her long stern face and her thin lips that never smiled. The widow of a colonel who had died just as he was on the point of becoming a general, the mother of a captain whom she had followed even in his campaigns, she had acquired a military stiffness of bearing and formed for herself a code of honor, duty and patriotism which kept her rigid, desiccated, as it were, by the stern application of discipline. She seldom, if ever, complained. When her son had become a widower after five years of married life she had undertaken the education of little Charles as a matter of course, performing her duties with the severity of a sergeant drilling recruits. She watched over the child, never tolerating the slightest waywardness or irregularity, but compelling him to sit up till midnight when his exercises were not finished, and sitting up herself until he had completed them. Under such implacable despotism Charles, whose constitution was delicate, grew up pale and thin, with beautiful eyes, inordinately large and clear, shining in his white, pinched face.

During the long hours of silence Mme Burle dwelt continuously upon one and the same idea: she had been disappointed in her son. This thought sufficed to occupy her mind, and under its influence she would live her whole life over again, from the birth of her son, whom she had pictured rising amid glory to the highest rank, till she came down to mean and narrow garrison life, the dull, monotonous existence of nowadays, that stranding in the post of a quartermaster, from which Burle would never rise and in which he seemed to sink more and more heavily. And yet his first efforts had filled her with pride, and she had hoped to see her dreams realized. Burle had only just left Saint-Cyr when he distinguished himself at the battle of Solferino, where he had captured a whole battery of the enemy's artillery with merely a handful of men. For this feat he had won the cross; the papers had recorded his heroism, and he had become known as one of the bravest soldiers in the army. But gradually the hero had grown stout, embedded in flesh, timorous, lazy and satisfied. In 1870, still a captain, he had been made a prisoner in the first encounter, and he returned from Germany quite furious, swearing that he would never be caught fighting again, for it was too absurd. Being prevented from leaving the army, as he was incapable of embracing any other profession, he applied for and obtained the position of captain quartermaster, "a kennel," as he called it, "in which he would be left to kick the bucket in peace." That day Mme Burle experienced a great internal disruption. She felt that it was all over, and she ever afterward preserved a rigid attitude with tightened lips.

A blast of wind shook the Rue des Recollets and drove the rain angrily against the windowpanes. The old lady lifted her eyes from the smoking vine roots now dying out, to make sure that Charles was not falling asleep over his Latin exercise. This lad, twelve years of age, had become the old lady's supreme hope, the one human being in whom she centered her obstinate yearning for glory. At first she had hated him with all the loathing she had felt for his mother, a weak and pretty young lacemaker whom the captain had been foolish enough to marry when he found out that she would not listen to his passionate addresses on any other condition. Later on, when the mother had died and the father had begun to wallow in vice, Mme Burle dreamed again in presence of that little ailing child whom she found it so hard to rear. She wanted to see him robust, so that he might grow into the hero that Burle had declined to be, and for all her cold ruggedness she watched him anxiously, feeling his limbs and instilling courage into his soul. By degrees, blinded by her passionate desires, she imagined that she had at last found the man of the family. The boy, whose temperament was of a gentle, dreamy character, had a physical horror of soldiering, but as he lived in mortal dread of his grandmother and was extremely shy and submissive, he would echo all she said and resignedly express his intention of entering the army when he grew up.

Mme Burle observed that the exercise was not progressing. In fact, little Charles, overcome by the deafening noise of the storm, was dozing, albeit his pen was between his fingers and his eyes were staring at the paper. The old lady at once struck the edge of the table with her bony hand; whereupon the lad started, opened his dictionary and hurriedly began to turn over the leaves. Then, still preserving silence, his grandmother drew the vine roots together on the hearth and unsuccessfully attempted to rekindle the fire.

At the time when she had still believed in her son she had sacrificed her small income, which he had squandered in pursuits she dared not investigate. Even now he drained the household; all its resources went to the streets, and it was through him that she lived in penury, with empty rooms and cold kitchen. She never spoke to him of all those things, for with her sense of discipline he remained the master. Only at times she shuddered at the sudden fear that Burle might someday commit some foolish misdeed which would prevent Charles from entering the army.

She was rising up to fetch a fresh piece of wood in the kitchen when a fearful hurricane fell upon the house, making the doors rattle, tearing off a shutter and whirling the water in the broken gutters like a spout against the window. In the midst of the uproar a ring at the bell startled the old lady. Who could it be at such an hour and in such weather? Burle never returned till after midnight, if he came home at all. However, she went to the door. An officer stood before her, dripping with rain and swearing savagely.

"Hell and thunder!" he growled. "What cursed weather!"

It was Major Laguitte, a brave old soldier who had served under Colonel Burle during Mme Burle's palmy days. He had started in life as a drummer boy and, thanks to his courage rather than his intellect, had attained to the command of a battalion, when a painful infirmity—the contraction of the muscles of one of his thighs, due to a wound—obliged him to accept the post of major. He was slightly lame, but it would have been imprudent to tell him so, as he refused to own it.

"What, you, Major?" said Mme Burle with growing astonishment.

"Yes, thunder," grumbled Laguitte, "and I must be confoundedly fond of you to roam the streets on such a night as this. One would think twice before sending even a parson out."

He shook himself, and little rivulets fell from his huge boots onto the floor. Then he looked round him.

"I particularly want to see Burle. Is the lazy beggar already in bed?"

"No, he is not in yet," said the old woman in her harsh voice.

The major looked furious, and, raising his voice, he shouted: "What, not at home? But in that case they hoaxed me at the cafe, Melanie's establishment, you know. I went there, and a maid grinned at me, saying that the captain had gone home to bed. Curse the girl! I suspected as much and felt like pulling her ears!"

After this outburst he became somewhat calmer, stamping about the room in an undecided way, withal seeming greatly disturbed. Mme Burle looked at him attentively.

"Is it the captain personally whom you want to see?" she said at last.

"Yes," he answered.

"Can I not tell him what you have to say?"

"No."

She did not insist but remained standing without taking her eyes off the major, who did not seem able to make up his mind to leave. Finally in a fresh burst of rage he exclaimed with an oath: "It can't be helped. As I am here you may as well know—after all, it is, perhaps, best."

He sat down before the chimney piece, stretching out his muddy boots as if a bright fire had been burning. Mme Burle was about to resume her own seat when she remarked that Charles, overcome by fatigue, had dropped his head between the open pages of his dictionary. The arrival of the major had at first interested him, but, seeing that he remained unnoticed, he had been unable to struggle against his sleepiness. His grandmother turned toward the table to slap his frail little hands, whitening in the lamplight, when Laguitte stopped her.

"No—no!" he said. "Let the poor little man sleep. I haven't got anything funny to say. There's no need for him to hear me."

The old lady sat down in her armchair; deep silence reigned, and they looked at one another.

"Well, yes," said the major at last, punctuating his words with an angry motion of his chin, "he has been and done it; that hound Burle has been and done it!"

Not a muscle of Mme Burle's face moved, but she became livid, and her figure stiffened. Then the major continued: "I had my doubts. I had intended mentioning the subject to you. Burle was spending too much money, and he had an idiotic look which I did not fancy. Thunder and lightning! What a fool a man must be to behave so filthily!"

Then he thumped his knee furiously with his clenched fist and seemed to choke with indignation. The old woman put the straightforward question:

"He has stolen?"

"You can't have an idea of it. You see, I never examined his accounts; I approved and signed them. You know how those things are managed. However, just before the inspection—as the colonel is a crotchety old maniac—I said to Burle: 'I say, old man, look to your accounts; I am answerable, you know,' and then I felt perfectly secure. Well, about a month ago, as he seemed queer and some nasty stories were circulating, I peered a little closer into the books and pottered over the entries. I thought everything looked straight and very well kept—"

At this point he stopped, convulsed by such a fit of rage that he had to relieve himself by a volley of appalling oaths. Finally he resumed: "It isn't the swindle that angers me; it is his disgusting behavior to me. He has gammoned me, Madame Burle. By God! Does he take me for an old fool?"

"So he stole?" the mother again questioned.

"This evening," continued the major more quietly, "I had just finished my dinner when Gagneux came in—you know Gagneux, the butcher at the corner of the Place aux Herbes? Another dirty beast who got the meat contract and makes our men eat all the diseased cow flesh in the neighborhood! Well, I received him like a dog, and then he let it all out—blurted out the whole thing, and a pretty mess it is! It appears that Burle only paid him in driblets and had got himself into a muddle—a confusion of figures which the devil himself couldn't disentangle. In short, Burle owes the butcher two thousand francs, and Gagneux threatens that he'll inform the colonel if he is not paid. To make matters worse, Burle, just to blind me, handed me every week a forged receipt which he had squarely signed with Gagneux's name. To think he did that to me, his old friend! Ah, curse him!"

With increasing profanity the major rose to his feet, shook his fist at the ceiling and then fell back in his chair. Mme Burle again repeated: "He has stolen. It was inevitable."

Then without a word of judgment or condemnation she added simply: "Two thousand francs—we have not got them. There are barely thirty francs in the house."

"I expected as much," said Laguitte. "And do you know where all the money goes? Why, Melanie gets it—yes, Melanie, a creature who has turned Burle into a perfect fool. Ah, those women! Those fiendish women! I always said they would do for him! I cannot conceive what he is made of! He is only five years younger than I am, and yet he is as mad as ever. What a woman hunter he is!"

Another long silence followed. Outside the rain was increasing in violence, and throughout the sleepy little town one could hear the crashing of slates and chimney pots as they were dashed by the blast onto the pavements of the streets.

"Come," suddenly said the major, rising, "my stopping here won't mend matters. I have warned you—and now I'm off."

"What is to be done? To whom can we apply?" muttered the old woman drearily.

"Don't give way—we must consider. If I only had the two thousand francs—but you know that I am not rich."

The major stopped short in confusion. This old bachelor, wifeless and childless, spent his pay in drink and gambled away at ecarte whatever money his cognac and absinthe left in his pocket. Despite that, however, he was scrupulously honest from a sense of discipline.

"Never mind," he added as he reached the threshold. "I'll begin by stirring him up. I shall move heaven and earth! What! Burle, Colonel Burle's son, condemned for theft! That cannot be! I would sooner burn down the town. Now, thunder and lightning, don't worry; it is far more annoying for me than for you."

He shook the old lady's hand roughly and vanished into the shadows of the staircase, while she held the lamp aloft to light the way. When she returned and replaced the lamp on the table she stood for a moment motionless in front of Charles, who was still asleep with his face lying on the dictionary. His pale cheeks and long fair hair made him look like a girl, and she gazed at him dreamily, a shade of tenderness passing over her harsh countenance. But it was only a passing emotion; her features regained their look of cold, obstinate determination, and, giving the youngster a sharp rap on his little hand, she said:

"Charles—your lessons."

The boy awoke, dazed and shivering, and again rapidly turned over the leaves. At the same moment Major Laguitte, slamming the house door behind him, received on his head a quantity of water falling from the gutters above, whereupon he began to swear in so loud a voice that he could be heard above the storm. And after that no sound broke upon the pelting downpour save the slight rustle of the boy's pen traveling over the paper. Mme Burle had resumed her seat near the chimney piece, still rigid, with her eyes fixed on the dead embers, preserving, indeed, her habitual attitude and absorbed in her one idea.

## CHAPTER II

## THE CAFE

The Cafe de Paris, kept by Melanie Cartier, a widow, was situated on the Place du Palais, a large irregular square planted with meager, dusty elm trees. The place was so well known in Vauchamp that it was customary to say, "Are you coming to Melanie's?" At the farther end of the first room, which was a spacious one, there was another called "the divan," a narrow apartment having sham leather benches placed against the walls, while at each corner there stood a marble-topped table. The widow, deserting her seat in the front room, where she left her little servant Phrosine, spent her evenings in the inner apartment, ministering to a few customers, the usual frequenters of the place, those who were currently styled "the gentlemen of the divan." When a man belonged to that set it was as if he had a label on his back; he was spoken of with smiles of mingled contempt and envy.

Mme Cartier had become a widow when she was five and twenty. Her husband, a wheelwright, who on the death of an uncle had amazed Vauchamp by taking the Cafe de Paris, had one fine day brought her back with him from Montpellier, where he was wont to repair twice a year to purchase liqueurs. As he was stocking his establishment he selected, together with divers beverages, a woman of the sort he wanted—of an engaging aspect and apt to stimulate the trade of the house. It was never known where he had picked her up, but he married her after trying her in the cafe during six months or so. Opinions were divided in Vauchamp as to her merits, some folks declaring that she was superb, while others asserted that she looked like a drum-major. She was a tall woman with large features and coarse hair falling low over her forehead. However, everyone agreed that she knew very well how to fool the sterner sex. She had fine eyes and was wont to fix them with a bold stare on the gentlemen of the divan, who colored and became like wax in her hands. She also had the reputation of possessing a wonderfully fine figure, and southerners appreciate a statuesque style of beauty.

Cartier had died in a singular way. Rumor hinted at a conjugal quarrel, a kick, producing some internal tumor. Whatever may have been the truth, Melanie found herself encumbered with the cafe, which was far from doing a prosperous business. Her husband had wasted his uncle's inheritance in drinking his own absinthe and wearing out the cloth of his own billiard table. For a while it was believed that the widow would have to sell out, but she liked the life and the establishment just as it was. If she could secure a few customers the bigger room might remain deserted. So she limited herself to repapering the divan in white and gold and recovering the benches. She began by entertaining a chemist. Then a vermicelli maker, a lawyer and a retired magistrate put in an appearance; and thus it was that the cafe remained open, although the waiter did not receive twenty orders a day. No objections were raised by the authorities, as appearances were kept up; and, indeed, it was not deemed advisable to interfere, for some respectable folks might have been worried.

Of an evening five or six well-to-do citizens would enter the front room and play at dominoes there. Although Cartier was dead and the Cafe de Paris had got a queer name, they saw nothing and kept up their old habits. In course of time, the waiter having nothing to do, Melanie dismissed him and made Phrosine light the solitary gas burner in the corner where the domino players congregated. Occasionally a party of young men, attracted by the gossip that circulated through the town, would come in, wildly excited and laughing loudly and awkwardly. But they were received there with icy dignity. As a rule they did not even see the widow, and even if she happened to be present she treated them with withering disdain, so that they withdrew, stammering and confused. Melanie was too astute to indulge in any compromising whims. While the front room remained obscure, save in the corner where the few townsfolk rattled their dominoes, she personally waited on the gentlemen of the divan, showing herself amiable without being free, merely venturing in moments of familiarity to lean on the shoulder of one or another of them, the better to watch a skillfully played game of ecarte.

One evening the gentlemen of the divan, who had ended by tolerating each other's presence, experienced a disagreeable surprise on finding Captain Burle at home there. He had casually entered the cafe that same morning to get a glass of vermouth, so it seemed, and he had found Melanie there. They had conversed, and in the evening when he returned Phrosine immediately showed him to the inner room.

Two days later Burle reigned there supreme; still he had not frightened the chemist, the vermicelli maker, the lawyer or the retired magistrate away. The captain, who was short and dumpy, worshiped tall, plump women. In his regiment he had been nicknamed "Petticoat Burle" on account of his constant philandering. Whenever the officers, and even the privates, met some monstrous-looking creature, some giantess puffed out with fat, whether she were in velvet or in rags, they would invariably exclaim, "There goes one to Petticoat Burle's taste!" Thus Melanie, with her opulent presence, quite conquered him. He was lost—quite wrecked. In less than a fortnight he had fallen to vacuous imbecility. With much the expression of a whipped hound in the tiny sunken eyes which lighted up his bloated face, he was incessantly watching the widow in mute adoration before her masculine features and stubby hair. For fear that he might be dismissed, he put up with the presence of the other gentlemen of the divan and spent his pay in the place down to the last copper. A sergeant reviewed the situation in one sentence: "Petticoat Burle is done for; he's a buried man!"

It was nearly ten o'clock when Major Laguitte furiously flung the door of the cafe open. For a moment those inside could see the deluged square transformed into a dark sea of liquid mud, bubbling under the terrible downpour. The major, now soaked to the skin and leaving a stream behind him, strode up to the small counter where Phrosine was reading a novel.

"You little wretch," he yelled, "you have dared to gammon an officer; you deserve—"

And then he lifted his hand as if to deal a blow such as would have felled an ox. The little maid shrank back, terrified, while the amazed domino players looked, openmouthed. However, the major did not linger there—he pushed the divan door open and appeared before Melanie and Burle just as the widow was playfully making the captain sip his grog in small spoonfuls, as if she were feeding a pet canary. Only the ex-magistrate and the chemist had come that evening, and they had retired early in a melancholy frame of mind. Then Melanie, being in want of three hundred francs for the morrow, had taken advantage of the opportunity to cajole the captain.

"Come." she said, "open your mouth; ain't it nice, you greedy piggy-wiggy?"

Burle, flushing scarlet, with glazed eyes and sunken figure, was sucking the spoon with an air of intense enjoyment.

"Good heavens!" roared the major from the threshold. "You now play tricks on me, do you? I'm sent to the roundabout and told that you never came here, and yet all the while here you are, addling your silly brains."

Burle shuddered, pushing the grog away, while Melanie stepped angrily in front of him as if to shield him with her portly figure, but Laguitte looked at her with that quiet, resolute expression well known to women who are familiar with bodily chastisement.

"Leave us," he said curtly.

She hesitated for the space of a second. She almost felt the gust of the expected blow, and then, white with rage, she joined Phrosine in the outer room.

When the two men were alone Major Laguitte walked up to Burle, looked at him and, slightly stooping, yelled into his face these two words: "You pig!"

The captain, quite dazed, endeavored to retort, but he had not time to do so.

"Silence!" resumed the major. "You have bamboozled a friend. You palmed off on me a lot of forged receipts which might have sent both of us to the gallows. Do you call that proper behavior? Is that the sort of trick to play a friend of thirty years' standing?"

Burle, who had fallen back in his chair, was livid; his limbs shook as if with ague. Meanwhile the major, striding up and down and striking the tables wildly with his fists, continued: "So you have become a thief like the veriest scribbling cur of a clerk, and all for the sake of that creature here! If at least you had stolen for your mother's sake it would have been honorable! But, curse it, to play tricks and bring the money into this shanty is what I cannot understand! Tell me— what are you made of at your age to go to the dogs as you are going all for the sake of a creature like a grenadier!"

"YOU gamble—" stammered the captain.

"Yes, I do—curse it!" thundered the major, lashed into still greater fury by this remark. "And I am a pitiful rogue to do so, because it swallows up all my pay and doesn't redound to the honor of the French army. However, I don't steal. Kill yourself, if it pleases you; starve your mother and the boy, but respect the regimental cashbox and don't drag your friends down with you."

He stopped. Burle was sitting there with fixed eyes and a stupid air. Nothing was heard for a moment save the clatter of the major's heels.

"And not a single copper," he continued aggressively. "Can you picture yourself between two gendarmes, eh?"

He then grew a little calmer, caught hold of Burle's wrists and forced him to rise.

"Come!" he said gruffly. "Something must be done at once, for I cannot go to bed with this affair on my mind—I have an idea."

In the front room Melanie and Phrosine were talking eagerly in low voices. When the widow saw the two men leaving the divan she moved toward Burle and said coaxingly: "What, are you going already, Captain?"

"Yes, he's going," brutally answered Laguitte, "and I don't intend to let him set foot here again."

The little maid felt frightened and pulled her mistress back by the skirt of her dress; in doing so she imprudently murmured the word "drunkard" and thereby brought down the slap which the major's hand had been itching to deal for some time past. Both women having stooped, however, the blow only fell on Phrosine's back hair, flattening her cap and breaking her comb. The domino players were indignant.

"Let's cut it," shouted Laguitte, and he pushed Burle on the pavement. "If I remained I should smash everyone in the place."

To cross the square they had to wade up to their ankles in mud. The rain, driven by the wind, poured off their faces. The captain walked on in silence, while the major kept on reproaching him with his cowardice and its disastrous consequences. Wasn't it sweet weather for tramping the streets? If he hadn't been such an idiot they would both be warmly tucked in bed instead of paddling about in the mud. Then he spoke of Gagneux—a scoundrel whose diseased meat had on three separate occasions made the whole regiment ill. In a week, however, the contract would come to an end, and the fiend himself would not get it renewed.

"It rests with me," the major grumbled. "I can select whomsoever I choose, and I'd rather cut off my right arm than put that poisoner in the way of earning another copper."

Just then he slipped into a gutter and, half choked by a string of oaths, he gasped:

"You understand—I am going to rout up Gagneux. You must stop outside while I go in. I must know what the rascal is up to and if he'll dare to carry out his threat of informing the colonel tomorrow. A butcher—curse him! The idea of compromising oneself with a butcher! Ah, you aren't over-proud, and I shall never forgive you for all this."

They had now reached the Place aux Herbes. Gagneux's house was quite dark, but Laguitte knocked so loudly that he was eventually admitted. Burle remained alone in the dense obscurity and did not even attempt to seek any shelter. He stood at a corner of the market under the pelting rain, his head filled with a loud buzzing noise which prevented him from thinking. He did not feel impatient, for he was unconscious of the flight of time. He stood there looking at the house, which, with its closed door and windows, seemed quite lifeless. When at the end of an hour the major came out again it appeared to the captain as if he had only just gone in.

Laguitte was so grimly mute that Burle did not venture to question him. For a moment they sought each other, groping about in the dark; then they resumed their walk through the somber streets, where the water rolled as in the bed of a torrent. They moved on in silence side by side, the major being so abstracted that he even forgot to swear. However, as they again crossed the Place du Palais, at the sight of the Cafe de Paris, which was still lit up, he dropped his hand on Burle's shoulder and said, "If you ever re-enter that hole I—"

"No fear!" answered the captain without letting his friend finish his sentence.

Then he stretched out his hand.

"No, no," said Laguitte, "I'll see you home; I'll at least make sure that you'll sleep in your bed tonight."

They went on, and as they ascended the Rue des Recollets they slackened their pace. When the captain's door was reached and Burle had taken out his latchkey he ventured to ask:

"Well?"

"Well," answered the major gruffly, "I am as dirty a rogue as you are. Yes! I have done a scurrilous thing. The fiend take you! Our soldiers will eat carrion for three months longer."

Then he explained that Gagneux, the disgusting Gagneux, had a horribly level head and that he had persuaded him—the major—to strike a bargain. He would refrain from informing the colonel, and he would even make a present of the two thousand francs and replace the forged receipts by genuine ones, on condition that the major bound himself to renew the meat contract. It was a settled thing.

"Ah," continued Laguitte, "calculate what profits the brute must make out of the meat to part with such a sum as two thousand francs."

Burle, choking with emotion, grasped his old friend's hands, stammering confused words of thanks. The vileness of the action committed for his sake brought tears into his eyes.

"I never did such a thing before," growled Laguitte, "but I was driven to it. Curse it, to think that I haven't those two thousand francs in my drawer! It is enough to make one hate cards. It is my own fault. I am not worth much; only, mark my words, don't begin again, for, curse it—I shan't."

The captain embraced him, and when he had entered the house the major stood a moment before the closed door to make certain that he had gone upstairs to bed. Then as midnight was striking and the rain was still belaboring the dark town, he slowly turned homeward. The thought of his men almost broke his heart, and, stopping short, he said aloud in a voice full of compassion:

"Poor devils! what a lot of cow beef they'll have to swallow for those two thousand francs!"

# CHAPTER III

AGAIN?

The regiment was altogether nonplused: Petticoat Burle had quarreled with Melanie. When a week had elapsed it became a proved and undeniable fact; the captain no longer set foot inside the Cafe de Paris, where the chemist, it was averred, once more reigned in his stead, to the profound sorrow of the retired magistrate. An even more incredible statement was that Captain Burle led the life of a recluse in the Rue des Recollets. He was becoming a reformed character; he spent his evenings at his own fireside, hearing little Charles repeat his lessons. His mother, who had never breathed a word to him of his manipulations with Gagneux, maintained her old severity of demeanor as she sat opposite to him in her armchair, but her looks seemed to imply that she believed him reclaimed.

A fortnight later Major Laguitte came one evening to invite himself to dinner. He felt some awkwardness at the prospect of meeting Burle again, not on his own account but because he dreaded awakening painful memories. However, as the captain was mending his ways he wished to shake hands and break a crust with him. He thought this would please his old friend.

When Laguitte arrived Burle was in his room, so it was the old lady who received the major. The latter, after announcing that he had come to have a plate of soup with them, added, lowering his voice:

"Well, how goes it?"

"It is all right," answered the old lady.

"Nothing queer?"

"Absolutely nothing. Never away—in bed at nine—and looking quite happy."

"Ah, confound it," replied the major, "I knew very well he only wanted a shaking. He has some heart left, the dog!"

When Burle appeared he almost crushed the major's hands in his grasp, and standing before the fire, waiting for the dinner, they conversed peacefully, honestly, together, extolling the charms of home life. The captain vowed he wouldn't exchange his home for a kingdom and declared that when he had removed his braces, put on his slippers and settled himself in his armchair, no king was fit to hold a candle to him. The major assented and examined him. At all events his virtuous conduct had not made him any thinner; he still looked bloated; his eyes were bleared, and his mouth was heavy. He seemed to be half asleep as he repeated mechanically: "Home life! There's nothing like home life, nothing in the world!"

"No doubt," said the major; "still, one mustn't exaggerate—take a little exercise and come to the cafe now and then."

"To the cafe, why?" asked Burle. "Do I lack anything here? No, no, I remain at home."

When Charles had laid his books aside Laguitte was surprised to see a maid come in to lay the cloth.

"So you keep a servant now," he remarked to Mme Burle.

"I had to get one," she answered with a sigh. "My legs are not what they used to be, and the household was going to rack and ruin. Fortunately Cabrol let me have his daughter. You know old Cabrol, who sweeps the market? He did not know what to do with Rose—I am teaching her how to work."

Just then the girl left the room.

"How old is she?" asked the major.

"Barely seventeen. She is stupid and dirty, but I only give her ten francs a month, and she eats nothing but soup."

When Rose returned with an armful of plates Laguitte, though he did not care about women, began to scrutinize her and was amazed at seeing so ugly a creature. She was very short, very dark and slightly deformed, with a face like an ape's: a flat nose, a huge mouth and narrow greenish eyes. Her broad back and long arms gave her an appearance of great strength.

"What a snout!" said Laguitte, laughing, when the maid had again left the room to fetch the cruets.

"Never mind," said Burle carelessly, "she is very obliging and does all one asks her. She suits us well enough as a scullion."

The dinner was very pleasant. It consisted of boiled beef and mutton hash. Charles was encouraged to relate some stories of his school, and Mme Burle repeatedly asked him the same question: "Don't you want to be a soldier?" A faint smile hovered over the child's wan lips as he answered with the frightened obedience of a trained dog, "Oh yes, Grandmother." Captain Burle, with his elbows on the table, was masticating slowly with an absent-minded expression. The big room was getting warmer; the single lamp placed on the table left the corners in vague gloom. There was a certain amount of heavy comfort, the familiar intimacy of penurious people who do not change their plates at every course but become joyously excited at the unexpected appearance of a bowl of whipped egg cream at the close of the meal.

Rose, whose heavy tread shook the floor as she paced round the table, had not yet opened her mouth. At last she stopped behind the captain's chair and asked in a gruff voice: "Cheese, sir?"

Burle started. "What, eh? Oh yes—cheese. Hold the plate tight."

He cut a piece of Gruyere, the girl watching him the while with her narrow eyes. Laguitte laughed; Rose's unparalleled ugliness amused him immensely. He whispered in the captain's ear, "She is ripping! There never was such a nose and such a mouth! You ought to send her to the colonel's someday as a curiosity. It would amuse him to see her."

More and more struck by this phenomenal ugliness, the major felt a paternal desire to examine the girl more closely.

"Come here," he said, "I want some cheese too."

She brought the plate, and Laguitte, sticking the knife in the Gruyere, stared at her, grinning the while because he discovered that she had one nostril broader than the other. Rose gravely allowed herself to be looked at, waiting till the gentleman had done laughing.

She removed the cloth and disappeared. Burle immediately went to sleep in the chimney corner while the major and Mme Burle began to chat. Charles had returned to his exercises. Quietude fell from the loft ceiling; the quietude of a middle-class household gathered in concord around their fireside. At nine o'clock Burle woke up, yawned and announced that he was going off to bed; he apologized but declared that he could not keep his eyes open. Half an hour later, when the major took his leave, Mme Burle vainly called for Rose to light him downstairs; the girl must have gone up to her room; she was, indeed, a regular hen, snoring the round of the clock without waking.

"No need to disturb anybody," said Laguitte on the landing; "my legs are not much better than yours, but if I get hold of the banisters I shan't break any bones. Now, my dear lady, I leave you happy; your troubles are ended at last. I watched Burle closely, and I'll take my oath that he's guileless as a child. Dash it—after all, it was high time for Petticoat Burle to reform; he was going downhill fast."

The major went away fully satisfied with the house and its inmates; the walls were of glass and could harbor no equivocal conduct. What particularly delighted him in his friend's return to virtue was that it absolved him from the obligation of verifying the accounts. Nothing was more distasteful to him than the inspection of a number of ledgers, and as long as Burle kept steady, he— Laguitte—could smoke his pipe in peace and sign the books in all confidence. However, he continued to keep one eye open for a little while longer and found the receipts genuine, the entries correct, the columns admirably balanced. A month later he contented himself with glancing at the receipts and running his eye over the totals. Then one morning, without the slightest suspicion of there being anything wrong, simply because he had lit a second pipe and had nothing to do, he carelessly added up a row of figures and fancied that he detected an error of thirteen francs. The balance seemed perfectly correct, and yet he was not mistaken; the total outlay was thirteen francs more than the various sums for which receipts were furnished. It looked queer, but he said nothing to Burle, just making up his mind to examine the next accounts closely. On the following week he detected a fresh error of nineteen francs, and then, suddenly becoming alarmed, he shut himself up with the books and spent a wretched morning poring over them, perspiring, swearing and feeling as if his very skull were bursting with the figures. At every page he discovered thefts of a few francs— the most miserable petty thefts—ten, eight, eleven francs, latterly, three and four; and, indeed, there was one column showing that Burle had pilfered just one franc and a half. For two months, however, he had been steadily robbing the cashbox, and by comparing dates the major found to his disgust that the famous lesson respecting Gagneux had only kept him straight for one week! This last discovery infuriated Laguitte, who struck the books with his clenched fists, yelling through a shower of oaths:

"This is more abominable still! At least there was some pluck about those forged receipts of Gagneux. But this time he is as contemptible as a cook charging twopence extra for her cabbages. Powers of hell! To pilfer a franc and a half and clap it in his pocket! Hasn't the brute got any pride then? Couldn't he run away with the safe or play the fool with actresses?"

The pitiful meanness of these pilferings revolted the major, and, moreover, he was enraged at having been duped a second time, deceived by the simple, stupid dodge of falsified additions. He rose at last and paced his office for a whole hour, growling aloud.

"This gives me his measure. Even if I were to thresh him to a jelly every morning he would still drop a couple of coins into his pocket every afternoon. But where can he spend it all? He is never seen abroad; he goes to bed at nine, and everything looks so clean and proper over there. Can the brute have vices that nobody knows of?"

He returned to the desk, added up the subtracted money and found a total of five hundred and forty-five francs. Where was this deficiency to come from? The inspection was close at hand, and if the crotchety colonel should take it into his head to examine a single page, the murder would be out and Burle would be done for.

This idea froze the major, who left off cursing, picturing Mme Burle erect and despairing, and at the same time he felt his heart swell with personal grief and shame.

"Well," he muttered, "I must first of all look into the rogue's business; I will act afterward."

As he walked over to Burle's office he caught sight of a skirt vanishing through the doorway. Fancying that he had a clue to the mystery, he slipped up quietly and listened and speedily recognized Melanie's shrill voice. She was complaining of the gentlemen of the divan. She had signed a promissory note which she was unable to meet; the bailiffs were in the house, and all her goods would be sold. The captain, however, barely replied to her. He alleged that he had no money, whereupon she burst into tears and began to coax him. But her blandishments were apparently ineffectual, for Burle's husky voice could be heard repeating, "Impossible! Impossible!" And finally the widow withdrew in a towering passion. The major, amazed at the turn affairs were taking, waited a few moments longer before entering the office, where Burle had remained alone. He found him very calm, and despite his furious inclination to call him names he also remained calm, determined to begin by finding out the exact truth.

The office certainly did not look like a swindler's den. A cane-seated chair, covered with an honest leather cushion, stood before the captain's desk, and in a corner there was the locked safe. Summer was coming on, and the song of a canary sounded through the open window. The apartment was very neat and tidy, redolent of old papers, and altogether its appearance inspired one with confidence.

"Wasn't it Melanie who was leaving here as I came along?" asked Laguitte.

Burle shrugged his shoulders.

"Yes," he mumbled. "She has been dunning me for two hundred francs, but she can't screw ten out of me—not even tenpence."

"Indeed!" said the major, just to try him. "I heard that you had made up with her."

"I? Certainly not. I have done with the likes of her for good."

Laguitte went away, feeling greatly perplexed. Where had the five hundred and forty-five francs gone? Had the idiot taken to drinking or gambling? He decided to pay Burle a surprise visit that very evening at his own house, and maybe by questioning his mother he might learn something. However, during the afternoon his leg became very painful; latterly he had been feeling in ill-health, and he had to use a stick so as not to limp too outrageously. This stick grieved him sorely, and he declared with angry despair that he was now no better than a pensioner. However, toward the evening, making a strong effort, he pulled himself out of his armchair and, leaning heavily on his stick, dragged himself through the darkness to the Rue des Recollets, which he reached about nine o'clock. The street door was still unlocked, and on going up he stood panting on the third landing, when he heard voices on the upper floor. One of these voices was Burle's, so he fancied, and out of curiosity he ascended another flight of stairs. Then at the end of a passage on the left he saw a ray of light coming from a door which stood ajar. As the creaking of his boots resounded, this door was sharply closed, and he found himself in the dark.

"Some cook going to bed!" he muttered angrily. "I'm a fool."

All the same he groped his way as gently as possible to the door and listened. Two people were talking in the room, and he stood aghast, for it was Burle and that fright Rose! Then he listened, and the conversation he heard left him no doubt of the awful truth. For a moment he lifted his stick as if to beat down the door. Then he shuddered and, staggering back, leaned against the wall. His legs were trembling under him, while in the darkness of the staircase he brandished his stick as if it had been a saber.

What was to be done? After his first moment of passion there had come thoughts of the poor old lady below. And these made him hesitate. It was all over with the captain now; when a man sank as low as that he was hardly worth the few shovelfuls of earth that are thrown over carrion to prevent them from polluting the atmosphere. Whatever might be said of Burle, however much one might try to shame him, he would assuredly begin the next day. Ah, heavens, to think of it! The money! The honor of the army! The name of Burle, that respected name, dragged through the mire! By all that was holy this could and should not be!

Presently the major softened. If he had only possessed five hundred and forty-five francs! But he had not got such an amount. On the previous day he had drunk too much cognac, just like a mere sub, and had lost shockingly at cards. It served him right—he ought to have known better! And if he was so lame he richly deserved it too; by rights, in fact, his leg ought to be much worse.

At last he crept downstairs and rang at the bell of Mme Burle's flat. Five minutes elapsed, and then the old lady appeared.

"I beg your pardon for keeping you waiting," she said; "I thought that dormouse Rose was still about. I must go and shake her."

But the major detained her.

"Where is Burle?" he asked.

"Oh, he has been snoring since nine o'clock. Would you like to knock at his door?"

"No, no, I only wanted to have a chat with you."

In the parlor Charles sat at his usual place, having just finished his exercises. He looked terrified, and his poor little white hands were tremulous. In point of fact, his grandmother, before sending him to bed, was wont to read some martial stories aloud so as to develop the latent family heroism in his bosom. That night she had selected the episode of the Vengeur, the man-of-war freighted with dying heroes and sinking into the sea. The child, while listening, had become almost hysterical, and his head was racked as with some ghastly nightmare.

Mme Burle asked the major to let her finish the perusal. "Long live the republic!" She solemnly closed the volume. Charles was as white as a sheet.

"You see," said the old lady, "the duty of every French soldier is to die for his country."

"Yes, Grandmother."

Then the lad kissed her on the forehead and, shivering with fear, went to bed in his big room, where the faintest creak of the paneling threw him into a cold sweat.

The major had listened with a grave face. Yes, by heavens! Honor was honor, and he would never permit that wretched Burle to disgrace the old woman and the boy! As the lad was so devoted to the military profession, it was necessary that he should be able to enter Saint-Cyr with his head erect.

When Mme Burle took up the lamp to show the major out, she passed the door of the captain's room, and stopped short, surprised to see the key outside, which was a most unusual occurrence.

"Do go in," she said to Laguitte; "it is bad for him to sleep so much."

And before he could interpose she had opened the door and stood transfixed on finding the room empty. Laguitte turned crimson and looked so foolish that she suddenly understood everything, enlightened by the sudden recollection of several little incidents to which she had previously attached no importance.

"You knew it—you knew it!" she stammered. "Why was I not told? Oh, my God, to think of it! Ah, he has been stealing again—I feel it!"

She remained erect, white and rigid. Then she added in a harsh voice:

"Look you—I wish he were dead!"

Laguitte caught hold of both her hands, which for a moment he kept tightly clasped in his own. Then he left her hurriedly, for he felt a lump rising in his throat and tears coming to his eyes. Ah, by all the powers, this time his mind was quite made up.

# CHAPTER IV

## INSPECTION

The regimental inspection was to take place at the end of the month. The major had ten days before him. On the very next morning, however, he crawled, limping, as far as the Cafe de Paris, where he ordered some beer. Melanie grew pale when she saw him enter, and it was with a lively recollection of a certain slap that Phrosine hastened to serve him. The major seemed very calm, however; he called for a second chair to rest his bad leg upon and drank his beer quietly like any other thirsty man. He had sat there for about an hour when he saw two officers crossing the Place du Palais—Morandot, who commanded one of the battalions of the regiment, and Captain Doucet. Thereupon he excitedly waved his cane and shouted: "Come in and have a glass of beer with me!"

The officers dared not refuse, but when the maid had brought the beer Morandot said to the major: "So you patronize this place now?"

"Yes—the beer is good."

Captain Doucet winked and asked archly: "Do you belong to the divan, Major?"

Laguitte chuckled but did not answer. Then the others began to chaff him about Melanie, and he took their remarks good-naturedly, simply shrugging his shoulders. The widow was undoubtedly a fine woman, however much people might talk. Some of those who disparaged her would, in reality, be only too pleased to win her good graces. Then turning to the little counter and assuming an engaging air, he shouted:

"Three more glasses, madame."

Melanie was so taken aback that she rose and brought the beer herself. The major detained her at the table and forgot himself so far as to softly pat the hand which she had carelessly placed on the back of a chair. Used as she was to alternate brutality and flattery, she immediately became confident, believing in a sudden whim of gallantry on the part of the "old wreck," as she was wont to style the major when talking with Phrosine. Doucet and Morandot looked at each other in surprise. Was the major actually stepping into Petticoat Burle's shoes? The regiment would be convulsed if that were the case.

Suddenly, however, Laguitte, who kept his eye on the square, gave a start.

"Hallo, there's Burle!" he exclaimed.

"Yes, it is his time," explained Phrosine. "The captain passes every afternoon on his way from the office."

In spite of his lameness the major had risen to his feet, pushing aside the chairs as he called out: "Burle! I say—come along and have a glass."

The captain, quite aghast and unable to understand why Laguitte was at the widow's, advanced mechanically. He was so perplexed that he again hesitated at the door.

"Another glass of beer," ordered the major, and then turning to Burle, he added, "What's the matter with you? Come in. Are you afraid of being eaten alive?"

The captain took a seat, and an awkward pause followed. Melanie, who brought the beer with trembling hands, dreaded some scene which might result in the closing of her establishment. The major's gallantry made her uneasy, and she endeavored to slip away, but he invited her to drink with them, and before she could refuse he had ordered Phrosine to bring a liqueur glass of anisette, doing so with as much coolness as if he had been master of the house. Melanie was thus compelled to sit down between the captain and Laguitte, who exclaimed aggressively: "I WILL have ladies respected. We are French officers! Let us drink Madame's health!"

Burle, with his eyes fixed on his glass, smiled in an embarrassed way. The two officers, shocked at the proceedings, had already tried to get off. Fortunately the cafe was deserted, save that the domino players were having their afternoon game. At every fresh oath which came from the major they glanced around, scandalized by such an unusual accession of customers and ready to threaten Melanie that they would leave her for the Cafe de la Gare if the soldiery was going to invade her place like flies that buzzed about, attracted by the stickiness of the tables which Phrosine scoured only on Saturdays. She was now reclining behind the counter, already reading a novel again.

"How's this—you are not drinking with Madame?" roughly said the major to Burle. "Be civil at least!"

Then as Doucet and Morandot were again preparing to leave, he stopped them.

"Why can't you wait? We'll go together. It is only this brute who never knows how to behave himself."

The two officers looked surprised at the major's sudden bad temper. Melanie attempted to restore peace and with a light laugh placed her hands on the arms of both men. However, Laguitte disengaged himself.

"No," he roared, "leave me alone. Why does he refuse to chink glasses with you? I shall not allow you to be insulted—do you hear? I am quite sick of him."

Burle, paling under the insult, turned slightly and said to Morandot, "What does this mean? He calls me in here to insult me. Is he drunk?"

With a wild oath the major rose on his trembling legs and struck the captain's cheek with his open hand. Melanie dived and thus escaped one half of the smack. An appalling uproar ensued. Phrosine screamed behind the counter as if she herself had received the blow; the domino players also entrenched themselves behind their table in fear lest the soldiers should draw their swords and massacre them. However, Doucet and Morandot pinioned the captain to prevent him from springing at the major's throat and forcibly let him to the door. When they got him outside they succeeded in quieting him a little by repeating that Laguitte was quite in the wrong. They would lay the affair before the colonel, having witnessed it, and the colonel would give his decision. As soon as they had got Burle away they returned to the cafe where they found

Laguitte in reality greatly disturbed, with tears in his eyes but affecting stolid indifference and slowly finishing his beer.

"Listen, Major," began Morandot, "that was very wrong on your part. The captain is your inferior in rank, and you know that he won't be allowed to fight you."

"That remains to be seen," answered the major.

"But how has he offended you? He never uttered a word. Two old comrades too; it is absurd."

The major made a vague gesture. "No matter. He annoyed me."

He could never be made to say anything else. Nothing more as to his motive was ever known. All the same, the scandal was a terrible one. The regiment was inclined to believe that Melanie, incensed by the captain's defection, had contrived to entrap the major, telling him some abominable stories and prevailing upon him to insult and strike Burle publicly. Who would have thought it of that old fogy Laguitte, who professed to be a woman hater? they said. So he, too, had been caught at last. Despite the general indignation against Melanie, this adventure made her very conspicuous, and her establishment soon drove a flourishing business.

On the following day the colonel summoned the major and the captain into his presence. He censured them sternly, accusing them of disgracing their uniform by frequenting unseemly haunts. What resolution had they come to, he asked, as he could not authorize them to fight? This same question had occupied the whole regiment for the last twenty-four hours. Apologies were unacceptable on account of the blow, but as Laguitte was almost unable to stand, it was hoped that, should the colonel insist upon it, some reconciliation might be patched up.

"Come," said the colonel, "will you accept me as arbitrator?"

"I beg your pardon, Colonel," interrupted the major; "I have brought you my resignation. Here it is. That settles everything. Please name the day for the duel."

Burle looked at Laguitte in amazement, and the colonel thought it his duty to protest.

"This is a most serious step, Major," he began. "Two years more and you would be entitled to your full pension."

But again did Laguitte cut him short, saying gruffly, "That is my own affair."

"Oh, certainly! Well, I will send in your resignation, and as soon as it is accepted I will fix a day for the duel."

The unexpected turn that events had taken startled the regiment. What possessed that lunatic major to persist in cutting the throat of his old comrade Burle? The officers again discussed Melanie; they even began to dream of her. There must surely be something wonderful about her since she had completely fascinated two such tough old veterans and brought them to a deadly feud. Morandot, having met Laguitte, did not disguise his concern. If he—the major—was not killed, what would he live upon? He had no fortune, and the pension to which his cross of the Legion of Honor entitled him, with the half of a full regimental pension which he would obtain on resigning, would barely find him in bread. While Morandot was thus speaking Laguitte simply stared before him with his round eyes, persevering in the dumb obstinacy born of his narrow mind; and when his companion tried to question him regarding his hatred for Burle, he simply made the same vague gesture as before and once again repeated:

"He annoyed me; so much the worse."

Every morning at mess and at the canteen the first words were: "Has the acceptance of the major's resignation arrived?" The duel was impatiently expected and ardently discussed. The majority believed that Laguitte would be run through the body in three seconds, for it was madness for a man to fight with a paralyzed leg which did not even allow him to stand upright. A few, however, shook their heads. Laguitte had never been a marvel of intellect, that was true; for the last twenty years, indeed, he had been held up as an example of stupidity, but there had been a time when he was known as the best fencer of the regiment, and although he had begun as a drummer he had won his epaulets as the commander of a battalion by the sanguine bravery of a man who is quite unconscious of danger. On the other hand, Burle fenced indifferently and passed for a poltroon. However, they would soon know what to think.

Meanwhile the excitement became more and more intense as the acceptance of Laguitte's resignation was so long in coming. The major was unmistakably the most anxious and upset of everybody. A week had passed by, and the general inspection would commence two days later. Nothing, however, had come as yet. He shuddered at the thought that he had, perhaps, struck his old friend and sent in his resignation all in vain, without delaying the exposure for a single minute. He had in reality reasoned thus: If he himself were killed he would not have the worry of witnessing the scandal, and if he killed Burle, as he expected to do, the affair would undoubtedly be hushed up. Thus he would save the honor of the army, and the little chap would be able to get in at Saint-Cyr. Ah, why wouldn't those wretched scribblers at the War Office hurry up a bit? The major could not keep still but was forever wandering about before the post office, stopping the estafettes and questioning the colonel's orderly to find out if the acceptance had arrived. He lost his sleep and, careless as to people's remarks, he leaned more and more heavily on his stick, hobbling about with no attempt to steady his gait.

On the day before that fixed for the inspection he was, as usual, on his way to the colonel's quarters when he paused, startled, to see Mme Burle (who was taking Charles to school) a few paces ahead of him. He had not met her since the scene at the Cafe de Paris, for she had remained in seclusion at home. Unmanned at thus meeting her, he stepped down to leave the whole sidewalk free. Neither he nor the old lady bowed, and the little boy lifted his large inquisitive eyes in mute surprise. Mme Burle, cold and erect, brushed past the major without the least sign of emotion or recognition. When she had passed he looked after her with an expression of stupefied compassion.

"Confound it, I am no longer a man," he growled, dashing away a tear.

When he arrived at the colonel's quarters a captain in attendance greeted him with the words: "It's all right at last. The papers have come."

"Ah!" murmured Laguitte, growing very pale.

And again he beheld the old lady walking on, relentlessly rigid and holding the little boy's hand. What! He had longed so eagerly for those papers for eight days past, and now when the scraps had come he felt his brain on fire and his heart lacerated.

The duel took place on the morrow, in the barrack yard behind a low wall. The air was keen, the sun shining brightly. Laguitte had almost to be carried to the ground; one of his seconds supported him on one side, while on the other he leaned heavily, on his stick. Burle looked half asleep; his face was puffy with unhealthy fat, as if he had spent a night of debauchery. Not a word was spoken. They were all anxious to have it over.

Captain Doucet crossed the swords of the two adversaries and then drew back, saying: "Set to, gentlemen."

Burle was the first to attack; he wanted to test Laguitte's strength and ascertain what he had to expect. For the last ten days the encounter had seemed to him a ghastly nightmare which he could not fathom. At times a hideous suspicion assailed him, but he put it aside with terror, for it meant death, and he refused to believe that a friend could play him such a trick, even to set things right. Besides, Laguitte's leg reassured him; he would prick the major on the shoulder, and then all would be over.

During well-nigh a couple of minutes the swords clashed, and then the captain lunged, but the major, recovering his old suppleness of wrist, parried in a masterly style, and if he had returned the attack Burle would have been pierced through. The captain now fell back; he was livid, for he felt that he was at the mercy of the man who had just spared him. At last he understood that this was an execution.

Laguitte, squarely poised on his infirm legs and seemingly turned to stone, stood waiting. The two men looked at each other fixedly. In Burle's blurred eyes there arose a supplication—a prayer for pardon. He knew why he was going to die, and like a child he promised not to transgress again. But the major's eyes remained implacable; honor had spoken, and he silenced his emotion and his pity.

"Let it end," he muttered between his teeth.

Then it was he who attacked. Like a flash of lightning his sword flamed, flying from right to left, and then with a resistless thrust it pierced the breast of the captain, who fell like a log without even a groan.

Laguitte had released his hold upon his sword and stood gazing at that poor old rascal Burle, who was stretched upon his back with his fat stomach bulging out.

"Oh, my God! My God!" repeated the major furiously and despairingly, and then he began to swear.

They led him away, and, both his legs failing him, he had to be supported on either side, for he could not even use his stick.

Two months later the ex-major was crawling slowly along in the sunlight down a lonely street of Vauchamp, when he again found himself face to face with Mme Burle and little Charles. They were both in deep mourning. He tried to avoid them, but he now only walked with difficulty, and they advanced straight upon him without hurrying or slackening their steps. Charles still had the same gentle, girlish, frightened face, and Mme Burle retained her stern, rigid demeanor, looking even harsher than ever.

As Laguitte shrank into the corner of a doorway to leave the whole street to them, she abruptly stopped in front of him and stretched out her hand. He hesitated and then took it and pressed it, but he trembled so violently that he made the old lady's arm shake. They exchanged glances in silence.

"Charles," said the boy's grandmother at last, "shake hands with the major." The boy obeyed without understanding. The major, who was very pale, barely ventured to touch the child's frail fingers; then, feeling that he ought to speak, he stammered out: "You still intend to send him to Saint-Cyr?"

"Of course, when he is old enough," answered Mme Burle.

But during the following week Charles was carried off by typhoid fever. One evening his grandmother had again read him the story of the Vengeur to make him bold, and in the night he had become delirious. The poor little fellow died of fright.

# THE DEATH OF OLIVIER BECAILLE

## CHAPTER I

### MY PASSING

It was on a Saturday, at six in the morning, that I died after a three days' illness. My wife was searching a trunk for some linen, and when she rose and turned she saw me rigid, with open eyes and silent pulses. She ran to me, fancying that I had fainted, touched my hands and bent over me. Then she suddenly grew alarmed, burst into tears and stammered:

"My God, my God! He is dead!"

I heard everything, but the sounds seemed to come from a great distance. My left eye still detected a faint glimmer, a whitish light in which all objects melted, but my right eye was quite bereft of sight. It was the coma of my whole being, as if a thunderbolt had struck me. My will was annihilated; not a fiber of flesh obeyed my bidding. And yet amid the impotency of my inert limbs my thoughts subsisted, sluggish and lazy, still perfectly clear.

My poor Marguerite was crying; she had dropped on her knees beside the bed, repeating in heart-rending tones:

"He is dead! My God, he is dead!"

Was this strange state of torpor, this immobility of the flesh, really death, although the functions of the intellect were not arrested? Was my soul only lingering for a brief space before it soared away forever? From my childhood upward I had been subject to hysterical attacks, and twice in early youth I had nearly succumbed to nervous fevers. By degrees all those who surrounded me had got accustomed to consider me an invalid and to see me sickly. So much so that I myself had forbidden my wife to call in a doctor when I had taken to my bed on the day of our arrival at the cheap lodging house of the Rue Dauphine in Paris. A little rest would soon set me right again; it was only the fatigue of the journey which had caused my intolerable weariness. And yet I was conscious of having felt singularly uneasy. We had left our province somewhat abruptly; we were very poor and had barely enough money to support ourselves till I drew my first month's salary in the office where I had obtained a situation. And now a sudden seizure was carrying me off!

Was it really death? I had pictured to myself a darker night, a deeper silence. As a little child I had already felt afraid to die. Being weak and compassionately petted by everyone, I had concluded that I had not long to live, that I should soon be buried, and the thought of the cold earth filled me with a dread I could not master—a dread which haunted me day and night. As I grew older the same terror pursued me. Sometimes, after long hours spent in reasoning with myself, I thought that I had conquered my fear. I reflected, "After all, what does it matter? One dies and all is over. It is the common fate; nothing could be better or easier."

I then prided myself on being able to look death boldly in the face, but suddenly a shiver froze my blood, and my dizzy anguish returned, as if a giant hand had swung me over a dark abyss. It was some vision of the earth returning and setting reason at naught. How often at night did I start up in bed, not knowing what cold breath had swept over my slumbers but clasping my despairing hands and moaning, "Must I die?" In those moments an icy horror would stop my pulses while an appalling vision of dissolution rose before me. It was with difficulty that I could get to sleep again. Indeed, sleep alarmed me; it so closely resembled death. If I closed my eyes they might never open again—I might slumber on forever.

I cannot tell if others have endured the same torture; I only know that my own life was made a torment by it. Death ever rose between me and all I loved; I can remember how the thought of it poisoned the happiest moments I spent with Marguerite. During the first months of our married life, when she lay sleeping by my side and I dreamed of a fair future for her and with her, the foreboding of some fatal separation dashed my hopes aside and embittered my delights. Perhaps we should be parted on the morrow—nay, perhaps in an hour's time. Then utter discouragement assailed me; I wondered what the bliss of being united availed me if it were to end in so cruel a disruption.

My morbid imagination reveled in scenes of mourning. I speculated as to who would be the first to depart, Marguerite or I. Either alternative caused me harrowing grief, and tears rose to my eyes at the thought of our shattered lives. At the happiest periods of my existence I often became a prey to grim dejection such as nobody could understand but which was caused by the thought of impending nihility. When I was most successful I was to general wonder most depressed. The fatal question, "What avails it?" rang like a knell in my ears. But the sharpest sting of this torment was that it came with a secret sense of shame, which rendered me unable to confide my thoughts to another. Husband and wife lying side by side in the darkened room may quiver with the same shudder and yet remain mute, for people do not mention death any more than they pronounce certain obscene words. Fear makes it nameless.

I was musing thus while my dear Marguerite knelt sobbing at my feet. It grieved me sorely to be unable to comfort her by telling her that I suffered no pain. If death were merely the annihilation of the flesh it had been foolish of me to harbor so much dread. I experienced a selfish kind of restfulness in which all my cares were forgotten. My memory had become extraordinarily vivid. My whole life passed before me rapidly like a play in which I no longer acted a part; it was a curious and enjoyable sensation—I seemed to hear a far-off voice relating my own history.

I saw in particular a certain spot in the country near Guerande, on the way to Piriac. The road turns sharply, and some scattered pine trees carelessly dot a rocky slope. When I was seven years old I used to pass through those pines with my father as far as a crumbling old house, where Marguerite's parents gave me pancakes. They were salt gatherers and earned a scanty livelihood by working the adjacent salt marshes. Then I remembered the school at Nantes, where I had grown up, leading a monotonous life within its ancient walls and yearning for the broad horizon of Guerande and the salt marshes stretching to the limitless sea widening under the sky.

Next came a blank—my father was dead. I entered the hospital as clerk to the managing board and led a dreary life with one solitary diversion: my Sunday visits to the old house on Piriac road. The saltworks were doing badly; poverty reigned in the land, and Marguerite's parents were nearly penniless. Marguerite, when merely a child, had been fond of me because I trundled her about in a wheelbarrow, but on the morning when I asked her in marriage she shrank from me with a frightened gesture, and I realized that she thought me hideous. Her parents, however, consented at once; they looked upon my offer as a godsend, and the daughter submissively acquiesced. When she became accustomed to the idea of marrying me she did not seem to dislike it so much. On our wedding day at Guerande the rain fell in torrents, and when we got home my bride had to take off her dress, which was soaked through, and sit in her petticoats.

That was all the youth I ever had. We did not remain long in our province. One day I found my wife in tears. She was miserable; life was so dull; she wanted to get away. Six months later I had saved a little money by taking in extra work after office hours, and through the influence of a friend of my father's I obtained a petty appointment in Paris. I started off to settle there with the dear little woman so that she might cry no more. During the night, which we spent in the third-class railway carriage, the seats being very hard, I took her in my arms in order that she might sleep.

That was the past, and now I had just died on the narrow couch of a Paris lodging house, and my wife was crouching on the floor, crying bitterly. The white light before my left eye was growing dim, but I remembered the room perfectly. On the left there was a chest of drawers, on the right a mantelpiece surmounted by a damaged clock without a pendulum, the hands of which marked ten minutes past ten. The window overlooked the Rue Dauphine, a long, dark street. All Paris seemed to pass below, and the noise was so great that the window shook.

We knew nobody in the city; we had hurried our departure, but I was not expected at the office till the following Monday. Since I had taken to my bed I had wondered at my imprisonment in this narrow room into which we had tumbled after a railway journey of fifteen hours, followed by a hurried, confusing transit through the noisy streets. My wife had nursed me with smiling tenderness, but I knew that she was anxious. She would walk to the window, glance out and return to the bedside, looking very pale and startled by the sight of the busy thoroughfare, the aspect of the vast city of which she did not know a single stone and which deafened her with its continuous roar. What would happen to her if I never woke up again—alone, friendless and unknowing as she was?

Marguerite had caught hold of one of my hands which lay passive on the coverlet, and, covering it with kisses, she repeated wildly: "Olivier, answer me. Oh, my God, he is dead, dead!"

So death was not complete annihilation. I could hear and think. I had been uselessly alarmed all those years. I had not dropped into utter vacancy as I had anticipated. I could not picture the disappearance of my being, the suppression of all that I had been, without the possibility of renewed existence. I had been wont to shudder whenever in any book or newspaper I came across a date of a hundred years hence. A date at which I should no longer be alive, a future which I should never see, filled me with unspeakable uneasiness. Was I not the whole world, and would not the universe crumble away when I was no more?

To dream of life had been a cherished vision, but this could not possibly be death. I should assuredly awake presently. Yes, in a few moments I would lean over, take Marguerite in my arms and dry her tears. I would rest a little while longer before going to my office, and then a new life would begin, brighter than the last. However, I did not feel impatient; the commotion had been too strong. It was wrong of Marguerite to give way like that when I had not even the strength to turn my head on the pillow and smile at her. The next time that she moaned out, "He is dead! Dead!" I would embrace her and murmur softly so as not to startle her: "No, my darling, I was only asleep. You see, I am alive, and I love you."

## CHAPTER II

## FUNERAL PREPARATIONS

Marguerite's cries had attracted attention, for all at once the door was opened and a voice exclaimed: "What is the matter, neighbor? Is he worse?"

I recognized the voice; it was that of an elderly woman, Mme Gabin, who occupied a room on the same floor. She had been most obliging since our arrival and had evidently become interested in our concerns. On her own side she had lost no time in telling us her history. A stern landlord had sold her furniture during the previous winter to pay himself his rent, and since then she had resided at the lodging house in the Rue Dauphine with her daughter Dede, a child of ten. They both cut and pinked lamp shades, and between them they earned at the utmost only two francs a day.

"Heavens! Is it all over?" cried Mme Gabin, looking at me.

I realized that she was drawing nearer. She examined me, touched me and, turning to Marguerite, murmured compassionately: "Poor girl! Poor girl!"

My wife, wearied out, was sobbing like a child. Mme Gabin lifted her, placed her in a dilapidated armchair near the fireplace and proceeded to comfort her.

"Indeed, you'll do yourself harm if you go on like this, my dear. It's no reason because your husband is gone that you should kill yourself with weeping. Sure enough, when I lost Gabin I was just like you. I remained three days without swallowing a morsel of food. But that didn't help me—on the contrary, it pulled me down. Come, for the Lord's sake, be sensible!"

By degrees Marguerite grew calmer; she was exhausted, and it was only at intervals that she gave way to a fresh flow of tears. Meanwhile the old woman had taken possession of the room with a sort of rough authority.

"Don't worry yourself," she said as she bustled about. "Neighbors must help each other. Luckily Dede has just gone to take the work home. Ah, I see your trunks are not yet all unpacked, but I suppose there is some linen in the chest of drawers, isn't there?"

I heard her pull a drawer open; she must have taken out a napkin which she spread on the little table at the bedside. She then struck a match, which made me think that she was lighting one of the candles on the mantelpiece and placing it near me as a religious rite. I could follow her movements in the room and divine all her actions.

"Poor gentleman," she muttered. "Luckily I heard you sobbing, poor dear!" Suddenly the vague light which my left eye had detected vanished. Mme Gabin had just closed my eyelids, but I had not felt her finger on my face. When I understood this I felt chilled.

The door had opened again, and Dede, the child of ten, now rushed in, calling out in her shrill voice: "Mother, Mother! Ah, I knew you would be here! Look here, there's the money—three francs and four sous. I took back three dozen lamp shades."

"Hush, hush! Hold your tongue," vainly repeated the mother, who, as the little girl chattered on, must have pointed to the bed, for I guessed that the child felt perplexed and was backing toward the door.

"Is the gentleman asleep?" she whispered.

"Yes, yes—go and play," said Mme Gabin.

But the child did not go. She was, no doubt, staring at me with widely opened eyes, startled and vaguely comprehending. Suddenly she seemed convulsed with terror and ran out, upsetting a chair.

"He is dead, Mother; he is dead!" she gasped.

Profound silence followed. Marguerite, lying back in the armchair, had left off crying. Mme Gabin was still rummaging about the room and talking under her breath.

"Children know everything nowadays. Look at that girl. Heaven knows how carefully she's brought up! When I send her on an errand or take the shades back I calculate the time to a minute so that she can't loiter about, but for all that she learns everything. She saw at a glance what had happened here—and yet I never showed her but one corpse, that of her uncle Francois, and she was then only four years old. Ah well, there are no children left—it can't be helped."

She paused and without any transition passed to another subject.

"I say, dearie, we must think of the formalities—there's the declaration at the municipal offices to be made and the seeing about the funeral. You are not in a fit state to attend to business. What do you say if I look in at Monsieur Simoneau's to find out if he's at home?"

Marguerite did not reply. It seemed to me that I watched her from afar and at times changed into a subtle flame hovering above the room, while a stranger lay heavy and unconscious on my bed. I wished that Marguerite had declined the assistance of Simoneau. I had seen him three or four times during my brief illness, for he occupied a room close to ours and had been civil and neighborly. Mme Gabin had told us that he was merely making a short stay in Paris, having come to collect some old debts due to his father, who had settled in the country and recently died. He was a tall, strong, handsome young man, and I hated him, perhaps on account of his healthy appearance. On the previous evening he had come in to make inquiries, and I had much disliked seeing him at Marguerite's side; she had looked so fair and pretty, and he had gazed so intently into her face when she smilingly thanked him for his kindness.

"Ah, here is Monsieur Simoneau," said Mme Gabin, introducing him.

He gently pushed the door ajar, and as soon as Marguerite saw him enter she burst into a flood of tears. The presence of a friend, of the only person she knew in Paris besides the old woman, recalled her bereavement. I could not see the young man, but in the darkness that encompassed me I conjured up his appearance. I pictured him distinctly, grave and sad at finding poor Marguerite in such distress. How lovely she must have looked with her golden hair unbound, her pale face and her dear little baby hands burning with fever!

"I am at your disposal, madame," he said softly. "Pray allow me to manage everything."

She only answered him with broken words, but as the young man was leaving, accompanied by Mme Gabin, I heard the latter mention money. These things were always expensive, she said, and she feared that the poor little body hadn't a farthing—anyhow, he might ask her. But Simoneau silenced the old woman; he did not want to have the widow worried; he was going to the municipal office and to the undertaker's.

When silence reigned once more I wondered if my nightmare would last much longer. I was certainly alive, for I was conscious of passing incidents, and I began to realize my condition. I must have fallen into one of those cataleptic states that I had read of. As a child I had suffered from syncopes which had lasted several hours, but surely my heart would beat anew, my blood circulate and my muscles relax. Yes, I should wake up and comfort Marguerite, and, reasoning thus, I tried to be patient.

Time passed. Mme Gabin had brought in some breakfast, but Marguerite refused to taste any food. Later on the afternoon waned. Through the open window I heard the rising clamor of the Rue Dauphine. By and by a slight ringing of the brass candlestick on the marble-topped table made me think that a fresh candle had been lighted. At last Simoneau returned.

"Well?" whispered the old woman.

"It is all settled," he answered; "the funeral is ordered for tomorrow at eleven. There is nothing for you to do, and you needn't talk of these things before the poor lady."

Nevertheless, Mme Gabin remarked: "The doctor of the dead hasn't come yet."

Simoneau took a seat beside Marguerite and after a few words of encouragement remained silent. The funeral was to take place at eleven! Those words rang in my brain like a passing bell. And the doctor coming—the doctor of the dead, as Mme Gabin had called him. HE could not possibly fail to find out that I was only in a state of lethargy; he would do whatever might be necessary to rouse me, so I longed for his arrival with feverish anxiety.

The day was drawing to a close. Mme Gabin, anxious to waste no time, had brought in her lamp shades and summoned Dede without asking Marguerite's permission. "To tell the truth," she observed, "I do not like to leave children too long alone."

"Come in, I say," she whispered to the little girl; "come in, and don't be frightened. Only don't look toward the bed or you'll catch it."

She thought it decorous to forbid Dede to look at me, but I was convinced that the child was furtively glancing at the corner where I lay, for every now and then I heard her mother rap her knuckles and repeat angrily: "Get on with your work or you shall leave the room, and the gentleman will come during the night and pull you by the feet."

The mother and daughter had sat down at our table. I could plainly hear the click of their scissors as they clipped the lamp shades, which no doubt required very delicate manipulation, for they did not work rapidly. I counted the shades one by one as they were laid aside, while my anxiety grew more and more intense.

The clicking of the scissors was the only noise in the room, so I concluded that Marguerite had been overcome by fatigue and was dozing. Twice Simoneau rose, and the torturing thought flashed through me that he might be taking advantage of her slumbers to touch her hair with his lips. I hardly knew the man and yet felt sure that he loved my wife. At last little Dede began to giggle, and her laugh exasperated me.

"Why are you sniggering, you idiot?" asked her mother. "Do you want to be turned out on the landing? Come, out with it; what makes you laugh so?"

The child stammered: she had not laughed; she had only coughed, but I felt certain she had seen Simoneau bending over Marguerite and had felt amused.

The lamp had been lit when a knock was heard at the door.

"It must be the doctor at last," said the old woman.

It was the doctor; he did not apologize for coming so late, for he had no doubt ascended many flights of stairs during the day. The room being but imperfectly lighted by the lamp, he inquired: "Is the body here?"

"Yes, it is," answered Simoneau.

Marguerite had risen, trembling violently. Mme Gabin dismissed Dede, saying it was useless that a child should be present, and then she tried to lead my wife to the window, to spare her the sight of what was about to take place.

The doctor quickly approached the bed. I guessed that he was bored, tired and impatient. Had he touched my wrist? Had he placed his hand on my heart? I could not tell, but I fancied that he had only carelessly bent over me.

"Shall I bring the lamp so that you may see better?" asked Simoneau obligingly.

"No it is not necessary," quietly answered the doctor.

Not necessary! That man held my life in his hands, and he did not think it worth while to proceed to a careful examination! I was not dead! I wanted to cry out that I was not dead!

"At what o'clock did he die?" asked the doctor.

"At six this morning," volunteered Simoneau.

A feeling of frenzy and rebellion rose within me, bound as I was in seemingly iron chains. Oh, for the power of uttering one word, of moving a single limb!

"This close weather is unhealthy," resumed the doctor; "nothing is more trying than these early spring days."

And then he moved away. It was like my life departing. Screams, sobs and insults were choking me, struggling in my convulsed throat, in which even my breath was arrested. The wretch! Turned into a mere machine by professional habits, he only came to a deathbed to accomplish a perfunctory formality; he knew nothing; his science was a lie, since he could not at a glance distinguish life from death—and now he was going—going!

"Good night, sir," said Simoneau.

There came a moment's silence; the doctor was probably bowing to Marguerite, who had turned while Mme Gabin was fastening the window. He left the room, and I heard his footsteps descending the stairs.

It was all over; I was condemned. My last hope had vanished with that man. If I did not wake before eleven on the morrow I should be buried alive. The horror of that thought was so great that I lost all consciousness of my surroundings—'twas something like a fainting fit in death. The last sound I heard was the clicking of the scissors handled by Mme Gabin and Dede. The funeral vigil had begun; nobody spoke.

Marguerite had refused to retire to rest in the neighbor's room. She remained reclining in her armchair, with her beautiful face pale, her eyes closed and her long lashes wet with tears, while before her in the gloom Simoneau sat silently watching her.

## CHAPTER III

## THE PROCESSION

I cannot describe my agony during the morning of the following day. I remember it as a hideous dream in which my impressions were so ghastly and so confused that I could not formulate them. The persistent yearning for a sudden awakening increased my torture, and as the hour for the funeral drew nearer my anguish became more poignant still.

It was only at daybreak that I had recovered a fuller consciousness of what was going on around me. The creaking of hinges startled me out of my stupor. Mme Gabin had just opened the window. It must have been about seven o'clock, for I heard the cries of hawkers in the street, the shrill voice of a girl offering groundsel and the hoarse voice of a man shouting "Carrots!" The clamorous awakening of Paris pacified me at first. I could not believe that I should be laid under the sod in the midst of so much life; and, besides, a sudden thought helped to calm me. It had just occurred to me that I had witnessed a case similar to my own when I was employed at the hospital of Guerande. A man had been sleeping twenty-eight hours, the doctors hesitating in presence of his apparent lifelessness, when suddenly he had sat up in bed and was almost at once able to rise. I myself had already been asleep for some twenty-five hours; if I awoke at ten I should still be in time.

I endeavored to ascertain who was in the room and what was going on there. Dede must have been playing on the landing, for once when the door opened I heard her shrill childish laughter outside. Simoneau must have retired, for nothing indicated his presence. Mme Gabin's slipshod tread was still audible over the floor. At last she spoke.

"Come, my dear," she said. "It is wrong of you not to take it while it is hot. It would cheer you up."

She was addressing Marguerite, and a slow trickling sound as of something filtering indicated that she had been making some coffee.

"I don't mind owning," she continued, "that I needed it. At my age sitting up IS trying. The night seems so dreary when there is a misfortune in the house. DO have a cup of coffee, my dear—just a drop."

She persuaded Marguerite to taste it.

"Isn't it nice and hot?" she continued, "and doesn't it set one up? Ah, you'll be wanting all your strength presently for what you've got to go through today. Now if you were sensible you'd step into my room and just wait there."

"No, I want to stay here," said Marguerite resolutely.

Her voice, which I had not heard since the previous evening, touched me strangely. It was changed, broken as by tears. To feel my dear wife near me was a last consolation. I knew that her eyes were fastened on me and that she was weeping with all the anguish of her heart.

The minutes flew by. An inexplicable noise sounded from beyond the door. It seemed as if some people were bringing a bulky piece of furniture upstairs and knocking against the walls as they did so. Suddenly I understood, as I heard Marguerite begin to sob; it was the coffin.

"You are too early," said Mme Gabin crossly. "Put it behind the bed."

What o'clock was it? Nine, perhaps. So the coffin had come. Amid the opaque night around me I could see it plainly, quite new, with roughly planed boards. Heavens! Was this the end then? Was I to be borne off in that box which I realized was lying at my feet?

However, I had one supreme joy. Marguerite, in spite of her weakness, insisted upon discharging all the last offices. Assisted by the old woman, she dressed me with all the tenderness of a wife and a sister. Once more I felt myself in her arms as she clothed me in various garments. She paused at times, overcome by grief; she clasped me convulsively, and her tears rained on my face. Oh, how I longed to return her embrace and cry, "I live!" And yet I was lying there powerless, motionless, inert!

"You are foolish," suddenly said Mme Gabin; "it is all wasted."

"Never mind," answered Marguerite, sobbing. "I want him to wear his very best things."

I understood that she was dressing me in the clothes I had worn on my wedding day. I had kept them carefully for great occasions. When she had finished she fell back exhausted in the armchair.

Simoneau now spoke; he had probably just entered the room.

"They are below," he whispered.

"Well, it ain't any too soon," answered Mme Gabin, also lowering her voice. "Tell them to come up and get it over."

"But I dread the despair of the poor little wife."

The old woman seemed to reflect and presently resumed: "Listen to me, Monsieur Simoneau. You must take her off to my room. I wouldn't have her stop here. It is for her own good. When she is out of the way we'll get it done in a jiffy."

These words pierced my heart, and my anguish was intense when I realized that a struggle was actually taking place. Simoneau had walked up to Marguerite, imploring her to leave the room.

"Do, for pity's sake, come with me!" he pleaded. "Spare yourself useless pain."

"No, no!" she cried. "I will remain till the last minute. Remember that I have only him in the world, and when he is gone I shall be all alone!"

From the bedside Mme Gabin was prompting the young man.

"Don't parley—take hold of her, carry her off in your arms."

Was Simoneau about to lay his hands on Marguerite and bear her away? She screamed. I wildly endeavored to rise, but the springs of my limbs were broken. I remained rigid, unable to lift my eyelids to see what was going on. The struggle continued, and my wife clung to the furniture, repeating, "Oh, don't, don't! Have mercy! Let me go! I will not—"

He must have lifted her in his stalwart arms, for I heard her moaning like a child. He bore her away; her sobs were lost in the distance, and I fancied I saw them both—he, tall and strong, pressing her to his breast; she, fainting, powerless and conquered, following him wherever he listed.

"Drat it all! What a to-do!" muttered Mme Gabin. "Now for the tug of war, as the coast is clear at last."

In my jealous madness I looked upon this incident as a monstrous outrage. I had not been able to see Marguerite for twenty-four hours, but at least I had still heard her voice. Now even this was denied me; she had been torn away; a man had eloped with her even before I was laid under the sod. He was alone with her on the other side of the wall, comforting her—embracing her, perhaps!

But the door opened once more, and heavy footsteps shook the floor.

"Quick, make haste," repeated Mme Gabin. "Get it done before the lady comes back."

She was speaking to some strangers, who merely answered her with uncouth grunts.

"You understand," she went on, "I am not a relation; I'm only a neighbor. I have no interest in the matter. It is out of pure good nature that I have mixed myself up in their affairs. And I ain't over cheerful, I can tell you. Yes, yes, I sat up the whole blessed night—it was pretty cold, too, about four o'clock. That's a fact. Well, I have always been a fool—I'm too soft-hearted."

The coffin had been dragged into the center of the room. As I had not awakened I was condemned. All clearness departed from my ideas; everything seemed to revolve in a black haze, and I experienced such utter lassitude that it seemed almost a relief to leave off hoping.

"They haven't spared the material," said one of the undertaker's men in a gruff voice. "The box is too long."

"He'll have all the more room," said the other, laughing.

I was not heavy, and they chuckled over it since they had three flights of stairs to descend. As they were seizing me by the shoulders and feet I heard Mme Gabin fly into a violent passion.

"You cursed little brat," she screamed, "what do you mean by poking your nose where you're not wanted? Look here, I'll teach you to spy and pry."

Dede had slipped her tousled head through the doorway to see how the gentleman was being put into the box. Two ringing slaps resounded, however, by an explosion of sobs. And as soon as the mother returned she began to gossip about her daughter for the benefit of the two men who were settling me in the coffin.

"She is only ten, you know. She is not a bad girl, but she is frightfully inquisitive. I do not beat her often; only I WILL be obeyed."

"Oh," said one of the men, "all kids are alike. Whenever there is a corpse lying about they always want to see it."

I was commodiously stretched out, and I might have thought myself still in bed, had it not been that my left arm felt a trifle cramped from being squeezed against a board. The men had been right. I was pretty comfortable inside on account of my diminutive stature.

"Stop!" suddenly exclaimed Mme Gabin. "I promised his wife to put a pillow under his head."

The men, who were in a hurry, stuffed in the pillow roughly. One of them, who had mislaid his hammer, began to swear. He had left the tool below and went to fetch it, dropping the lid, and when two sharp blows of the hammer drove in the first nail, a shock ran through my being—I had ceased to live. The nails then entered in rapid succession with a rhythmical cadence. It was as if some packers had been closing a case of dried fruit with easy dexterity. After that such sounds as reached me were deadened and strangely prolonged, as if the deal coffin had been changed into a huge musical box. The last words spoken in the room of the Rue Dauphine—at least the last ones that I heard distinctly— were uttered by Mme Gabin.

"Mind the staircase," she said; "the banister of the second flight isn't safe, so be careful."

While I was being carried down I experienced a sensation similar to that of pitching as when one is on board a ship in a rough sea. However, from that moment my impressions became more and more vague. I remember that the only distinct thought that still possessed me was an imbecile, impulsive curiosity as to the road by which I should be taken to the cemetery. I was not acquainted with a single street of Paris, and I was ignorant of the position of the large burial grounds (though of course I had occasionally heard their names), and yet every effort of my mind was directed toward ascertaining whether we were turning to the right or to the left. Meanwhile the jolting of the hearse over the paving stones, the rumbling of passing vehicles, the steps of the foot passengers, all created a confused clamor, intensified by the acoustical properties of the coffin.

At first I followed our course pretty closely; then came a halt. I was again lifted and carried about, and I concluded that we were in church, but when the funeral procession once more moved onward I lost all consciousness of the road we took. A ringing of bells informed me that we were passing another church, and then the softer and easier progress of the wheels indicated that we were skirting a garden or park. I was like a victim being taken to the gallows, awaiting in stupor a deathblow that never came.

At last they stopped and pulled me out of the hearse. The business proceeded rapidly. The noises had ceased; I knew that I was in a deserted space amid avenues of trees and with the broad sky over my head. No doubt a few persons followed the bier, some of the inhabitants of the lodging house, perhaps—Simoneau and others, for instance—for faint whisperings reached my ear. Then I heard a psalm chanted and some Latin words mumbled by a priest, and afterward I suddenly felt myself sinking, while the ropes rubbing against the edges of the coffin elicited lugubrious sounds, as if a bow were being drawn across the strings of a cracked violoncello. It was the end. On the left side of my head I felt a violent shock like that produced by the bursting of a bomb, with another under my feet and a third more violent still on my chest. So forcible, indeed, was this last one that I thought the lid was cleft atwain. I fainted from it.

# CHAPTER IV

## THE NAIL

It is impossible for me to say how long my swoon lasted. Eternity is not of longer duration than one second spent in nihility. I was no more. It was slowly and confusedly that I regained some degree of consciousness. I was still asleep, but I began to dream; a nightmare started into shape amid the blackness of my horizon, a nightmare compounded of a strange fancy which in other days had haunted my morbid imagination whenever with my propensity for dwelling upon hideous thoughts I had conjured up catastrophes.

Thus I dreamed that my wife was expecting me somewhere—at Guerande, I believe—and that I was going to join her by rail. As we passed through a tunnel a deafening roll thundered over our head, and a sudden subsidence blocked up both issues of the tunnel, leaving our train intact in the center. We were walled up by blocks of rock in the heart of a mountain. Then a long and fearful agony commenced. No assistance could possibly reach us; even with powerful engines and incessant labor it would take a month to clear the tunnel. We were prisoners there with no outlet, and so our death was only a question of time.

My fancy had often dwelt on that hideous drama and had constantly varied the details and touches. My actors were men, women and children; their number increased to hundreds, and they were ever furnishing me with new incidents. There were some provisions in the train, but these were soon exhausted, and the hungry passengers, if they did not actually devour human flesh, at least fought furiously over the last piece of bread. Sometimes an aged man was driven back with blows and slowly perished; a mother struggled like a she-wolf to keep three or four mouthfuls for her child. In my own compartment a bride and bridegroom were dying, clasped in each other's arms in mute despair.

The line was free along the whole length of the train, and people came and went, prowling round the carriages like beasts of prey in search of carrion. All classes were mingled together. A millionaire, a high functionary, it was said, wept on a workman's shoulder. The lamps had been extinguished from the first, and the engine fire was nearly out. To pass from one carriage to another it was necessary to grope about, and thus, too, one slowly reached the engine, recognizable by its enormous barrel, its cold, motionless flanks, its useless strength, its grim silence, in the overwhelming night. Nothing could be more appalling than this train entombed alive with its passengers perishing one by one.

I gloated over the ghastliness of each detail; howls resounded through the vault; somebody whom one could not see, whose vicinity was not even suspected, would suddenly drop upon another's shoulder. But what affected me most of all was the cold and the want of air. I have never felt so chilled; a mantle of snow seemed to enwrap me; heavy moisture rained upon my skull; I was gasping; the rocky vault seemed to crush my chest; the whole mountain was seemingly weighing upon me.

Suddenly a cry of deliverance sounded. For some time past we fancied that we could hear a dull sound, and we tried to hope that men were at work and that help was coming, but it came not thus. One of the passengers, however, had discovered an air shaft in the tunnel, and, crowding round, we all saw this shaft, above which we could discern a blue patch about the size of a wafer. That blue patch filled us with rapture, for it was the sky. We stretched ourselves and stood on tiptoes to breathe more freely. Then we distinguished some black specks moving about, specks that must surely be workmen about to deliver us. A furious clamor arose. The cry "Saved! Saved!" burst from every mouth, while trembling arms were uplifted toward the tiny azure patch above.

That roar of voices aroused me. Where was I? In the tunnel, of course. I was lying at full length; hard walls were pressing against my ribs. Then I attempted to rise and struck my head roughly. Was it the rock closing in on all sides? The blue speck had vanished—aye, the sky had disappeared and I was still suffocating, shivering, with chattering teeth.

All at once I remembered. Intense horror raised my hair on end. I felt the hideous truth freeze me from head to foot like ice. I had shaken off the long coma which for many hours had stricken me with corpselike rigidity. Yes, I could move; my hands could feel the boards of my coffin; my lips parted; words came to me, and instinctively I called out Marguerite's name. It was a scream I raised. In that deal box my voice took so hoarse and weird a sound that it terrified me. Oh, my God, was this thing true? I was able to walk, speak, cry out that I was living, and yet my voice could not be heard; I was entombed under the earth.

I made a desperate effort to remain calm and reflect. Was there no means of getting out? Then my dream began afresh in my troubled brain. The fanciful air shaft with the blue bit of sky overhead was mingled with the real grave in which I was lying. I stared at the darkness with widely opened eyes; perhaps I might discover a hole, a slit, a glimmer of light, but only sparks of fire flitted through that night, with rays that broadened and then faded away. I was in a somber abyss again. With returning lucidity I struggled against these fatal visions. Indeed, I should need all my reason if I meant to try to save myself.

The most immediate peril lay in an increasing sense of suffocation. If I had been able to live so long without air it was owing to suspended animation, which had changed all the normal conditions of my existence, but now that my heart beat and my lungs breathed I should die, asphyxiated, if I did not promptly liberate myself. I also suffered from cold and dreaded lest I should succumb to the mortal numbness of those who fall asleep in the snow, never to wake again. Still, while unceasingly realizing the necessity of remaining calm, I felt maddening blasts sweep through my brain, and to quiet my senses I exhorted myself to patience, trying to remember the circumstances of my burial. Probably the ground had been bought for five years, and this would be against my chances of self-deliverance, for I remembered having noticed at Nantes that in the trenches of the common graves one end of the last lowered coffins protruded into the next open cavity, in which case I should only have had to break through one plank. But if I were in a separate hole, filled up above me with earth, the obstacles would prove too great. Had I not been told that the dead were buried six feet deep in Paris? How was I to get through the enormous mass of soil above me? Even if I succeeded in slitting the lid of my bier open the mold would drift in like fine sand and fill my mouth and eyes. That would be death again, a ghastly death, like drowning in mud.

However, I began to feel the planks carefully. The coffin was roomy, and I found that I was able to move my arms with tolerable ease. On both sides the roughly planed boards were stout and resistive. I slipped my arm onto my chest to raise it over my head. There I discovered in the top plank a knot in the wood which yielded slightly at my pressure. Working laboriously, I finally succeeded in driving out this knot, and on passing my finger through the hole I found that the earth was wet and clayey. But that availed me little. I even regretted having removed the knot, vaguely dreading the irruption of the mold. A second experiment occupied me for a while. I tapped all over the coffin to ascertain if perhaps there were any vacuum outside. But the sound was everywhere the same. At last, as I was slightly kicking the foot of the coffin, I fancied that it gave out a clearer echoing noise, but that might merely be produced by the sonority of the wood.

At any rate, I began to press against the boards with my arms and my closed fists. In the same way, too, I used my knees, my back and my feet without eliciting even a creak from the wood. I strained with all my strength, indeed, with so desperate an effort of my whole frame, that my bruised bones seemed breaking. But nothing moved, and I became insane.

Until that moment I had held delirium at bay. I had mastered the intoxicating rage which was mounting to my head like the fumes of alcohol; I had silenced my screams, for I feared that if I again cried out aloud I should be undone. But now I yelled; I shouted; unearthly howls which I could not repress came from my relaxed throat. I called for help in a voice that I did not recognize, growing wilder with each fresh appeal and crying out that I would not die. I also tore at the wood with my nails; I writhed with the contortions of a caged wolf. I do not know how long this fit of madness lasted, but I can still feel the relentless hardness of the box that imprisoned me; I can still hear the storm of shrieks and sobs with which I filled it; a remaining glimmer of reason made me try to stop, but I could not do so.

Great exhaustion followed. I lay waiting for death in a state of somnolent pain. The coffin was like stone, which no effort could break, and the conviction that I was powerless left me unnerved, without courage to make any fresh attempts. Another suffering—hunger—was presently added to cold and want of air. The torture soon became intolerable. With my finger I tried to pull small pinches of earth through the hole of the dislodged knot, and I swallowed them eagerly, only increasing my torment. Tempted by my flesh, I bit my arms and sucked my skin with a fiendish desire to drive my teeth in, but I was afraid of drawing blood.

Then I ardently longed for death. All my life long I had trembled at the thought of dissolution, but I had come to yearn for it, to crave for an everlasting night that could never be dark enough. How childish it had been of me to dread the long, dreamless sleep, the eternity of silence and gloom! Death was kind, for in suppressing life it put an end to suffering. Oh, to sleep like the stones, to be no more!

With groping hands I still continued feeling the wood, and suddenly I pricked my left thumb. That slight pain roused me from my growing numbness. I felt again and found a nail—a nail which the undertaker's men had driven in crookedly and which had not caught in the lower wood. It was long and very sharp; the head was secured to the lid, but it moved. Henceforth I had but one idea—to possess myself of that nail—and I slipped my right hand across my body and began to shake it. I made but little progress, however; it was a difficult job, for my hands soon tired, and I had to use them alternately. The left one, too, was of little use on account of the nail's awkward position.

While I was obstinately persevering a plan dawned on my mind. That nail meant salvation, and I must have it. But should I get it in time? Hunger was torturing me; my brain was swimming; my limbs were losing their strength; my mind was becoming confused. I had sucked the drops that trickled from my punctured finger, and suddenly I bit my arm and drank my own blood! Thereupon, spurred on by pain, revived by the tepid, acrid liquor that moistened my lips, I tore desperately at the nail and at last I wrenched it off!

I then believed in success. My plan was a simple one; I pushed the point of the nail into the lid, dragging it along as far as I could in a straight line and working it so as to make a slit in the wood. My fingers stiffened, but I doggedly persevered, and when I fancied that I had sufficiently cut into the board I turned on my stomach and, lifting myself on my knees and elbows thrust the whole strength of my back against the lid. But although it creaked it did not yield; the notched line was not deep enough. I had to resume my old position—which I only managed to do with infinite trouble—and work afresh. At last after another supreme effort the lid was cleft from end to end.

I was not saved as yet, but my heart beat with renewed hope. I had ceased pushing and remained motionless, lest a sudden fall of earth should bury me. I intended to use the lid as a screen and, thus protected, to open a sort of shaft in the clayey soil. Unfortunately I was assailed by unexpected difficulties. Some heavy clods of earth weighed upon the boards and made them unmanageable; I foresaw that I should never reach the surface in that way, for the mass of soil was already bending my spine and crushing my face.

Once more I stopped, affrighted; then suddenly, while I was stretching my legs, trying to find something firm against which I might rest my feet, I felt the end board of the coffin yielding. I at once gave a desperate kick with my heels in the faint hope that there might be a freshly dug grave in that direction.

It was so. My feet abruptly forced their way into space. An open grave was there; I had only a slight partition of earth to displace, and soon I rolled into the cavity. I was saved!

I remained for a time lying on my back in the open grave, with my eyes raised to heaven. It was dark; the stars were shining in a sky of velvety blueness. Now and then the rising breeze wafted a springlike freshness, a perfume of foliage, upon me. I was saved! I could breathe; I felt warm, and I wept and I stammered, with my arms prayerfully extended toward the starry sky. O God, how sweet seemed life!

# CHAPTER V

## MY RESURRECTION

My first impulse was to find the custodian of the cemetery and ask him to have me conducted home, but various thoughts that came to me restrained me from following that course. My return would create general alarm; why should I hurry now that I was master of the situation? I felt my limbs; I had only an insignificant wound on my left arm, where I had bitten myself, and a slight feverishness lent me unhoped-for strength. I should no doubt be able to walk unaided.

Still I lingered; all sorts of dim visions confused my mind. I had felt beside me in the open grave some sextons' tools which had been left there, and I conceived a sudden desire to repair the damage I had done, to close up the hole through which I had crept, so as to conceal all traces of my resurrection. I do not believe that I had any positive motive in doing so. I only deemed it useless to proclaim my adventure aloud, feeling ashamed to find myself alive when the whole world thought me dead. In half an hour every trace of my escape was obliterated, and then I climbed out of the hole.

The night was splendid, and deep silence reigned in the cemetery; the black trees threw motionless shadows over the white tombs. When I endeavored to ascertain my bearings I noticed that one half of the sky was ruddy, as if lit by a huge conflagration; Paris lay in that direction, and I moved toward it, following a long avenue amid the darkness of the branches.

However, after I had gone some fifty yards I was compelled to stop, feeling faint and weary. I then sat down on a stone bench and for the first time looked at myself. I was fully attired with the exception that I had no hat. I blessed my beloved Marguerite for the pious thought which had prompted her to dress me in my best clothes—those which I had worn at our wedding. That remembrance of my wife brought me to my feet again. I longed to see her without delay.

At the farther end of the avenue I had taken a wall arrested my progress. However, I climbed to the top of a monument, reached the summit of the wall and then dropped over the other side. Although roughly shaken by the fall, I managed to walk for a few minutes along a broad deserted street skirting the cemetery. I had no notion as to where I might be, but with the reiteration of monomania I kept saying to myself that I was going toward Paris and that I should find the Rue Dauphine somehow or other. Several people passed me but, seized with sudden distrust, I would not stop them and ask my way. I have since realized that I was then in a burning fever and already nearly delirious. Finally, just as I reached a large thoroughfare, I became giddy and fell heavily upon the pavement.

Here there is a blank in my life. For three whole weeks I remained unconscious. When I awoke at last I found myself in a strange room. A man who was nursing me told me quietly that he had picked me up one morning on the Boulevard Montparnasse and had brought me to his house. He was an old doctor who had given up practicing.

When I attempted to thank him he sharply answered that my case had seemed a curious one and that he had wished to study it. Moreover, during the first days of my convalescence he would not allow me to ask a single question, and later on he never put one to me. For eight days longer I remained in bed, feeling very weak and not even trying to remember, for memory was a weariness and a pain. I felt half ashamed and half afraid. As soon as I could leave the house I would go and find out whatever I wanted to know. Possibly in the delirium of fever a name had escaped me; however, the doctor never alluded to anything I may have said. His charity was not only generous; it was discreet.

The summer had come at last, and one warm June morning I was permitted to take a short walk. The sun was shining with that joyous brightness which imparts renewed youth to the streets of old Paris. I went along slowly, questioning the passers-by at every crossing I came to and asking the way to Rue Dauphine. When I reached the street I had some difficulty in recognizing the lodging house where we had alighted on our arrival in the capital. A childish terror made me hesitate. If I appeared suddenly before Marguerite the shock might kill her. It might be wiser to begin by revealing myself to our neighbor Mme Gabin; still I shrank from taking a third party into confidence. I seemed unable to arrive at a resolution, and yet in my innermost heart I felt a great void, like that left by some sacrifice long since consummated.

The building looked quite yellow in the sunshine. I had just recognized it by a shabby eating house on the ground floor, where we had ordered our meals, having them sent up to us. Then I raised my eyes to the last window of the third floor on the left-hand side, and as I looked at it a young woman with tumbled hair, wearing a loose dressing gown, appeared and leaned her elbows on the sill. A young man followed and printed a kiss upon her neck. It was not Marguerite. Still I felt no surprise. It seemed to me that I had dreamed all this with other things, too, which I was to learn presently.

For a moment I remained in the street, uncertain whether I had better go upstairs and question the lovers, who were still laughing in the sunshine. However, I decided to enter the little restaurant below. When I started on my walk the old doctor had placed a five-franc piece in my hand. No doubt I was changed beyond recognition, for my beard had grown during the brain fever, and my face was wrinkled and haggard. As I took a seat at a small table I saw Mme Gabin come in carrying a cup; she wished to buy a penny-worth of coffee. Standing in front of the counter, she began to gossip with the landlady of the establishment.

"Well," asked the latter, "so the poor little woman of the third floor has made up her mind at last, eh?"

"How could she help herself?" answered Mme Gabin. "It was the very best thing for her to do. Monsieur Simoneau showed her so much kindness. You see, he had finished his business in Paris to his satisfaction, for he has inherited a pot of money. Well, he offered to take her away with him to his own part of the country and place her with an aunt of his, who wants a housekeeper and companion."

The landlady laughed archly. I buried my face in a newspaper which I picked off the table. My lips were white and my hands shook.

"It will end in a marriage, of course," resumed Mme Gabin. "The little widow mourned for her husband very properly, and the young man was extremely well behaved. Well, they left last night—and, after all, they were free to please themselves."

Just then the side door of the restaurant, communicating with the passage of the house, opened, and Dede appeared.

"Mother, ain't you coming?" she cried. "I'm waiting, you know; do be quick."

"Presently," said the mother testily. "Don't bother."

The girl stood listening to the two women with the precocious shrewdness of a child born and reared amid the streets of Paris.

"When all is said and done," explained Mme Gabin, "the dear departed did not come up to Monsieur Simoneau. I didn't fancy him overmuch; he was a puny sort of a man, a poor, fretful fellow, and he hadn't a penny to bless himself with. No, candidly, he wasn't the kind of husband for a young and healthy wife, whereas Monsieur Simoneau is rich, you know, and as strong as a Turk."

"Oh yes!" interrupted Dede. "I saw him once when he was washing—his door was open. His arms are so hairy!"

"Get along with you," screamed the old woman, shoving the girl out of the restaurant. "You are always poking your nose where it has no business to be."

Then she concluded with these words: "Look here, to my mind the other one did quite right to take himself off. It was fine luck for the little woman!"

When I found myself in the street again I walked along slowly with trembling limbs. And yet I was not suffering much; I think I smiled once at my shadow in the sun. It was quite true. I WAS very puny. It had been a queer notion of mine to marry Marguerite. I recalled her weariness at Guerande, her impatience, her dull, monotonous life. The dear creature had been very good to me, but I had never been a real lover; she had mourned for me as a sister for her brother, not otherwise. Why should I again disturb her life? A dead man is not jealous.

When I lifted my eyelids I saw the garden of the Luxembourg before me. I entered it and took a seat in the sun, dreaming with a sense of infinite restfulness. The thought of Marguerite stirred me softly. I pictured her in the provinces, beloved, petted and very happy. She had grown handsomer, and she was the mother of three boys and two girls. It was all right. I had behaved like an honest man in dying, and I would not commit the cruel folly of coming to life again.

Since then I have traveled a good deal. I have been a little everywhere. I am an ordinary man who has toiled and eaten like anybody else. Death no longer frightens me, but it does not seem to care for me now that I have no motive in living, and I sometimes fear that I have been forgotten upon earth.

# Echo Library
## www.echo-library.com

Echo Library uses advanced digital print-on-demand technology to build and preserve an exciting world class collection of rare and out-of-print books, making them readily available for everyone to enjoy.

Situated just yards from Teddington Lock on the River Thames, Echo Library was founded in 2005 by Tom Cherrington, a specialist dealer in rare and antiquarian books with a passion for literature.

Please visit our website for a complete catalogue of our books, which includes foreign language titles.

### The Right to Read

Echo Library actively supports the Royal National Institute of the Blind's Right to Read initiative by publishing a comprehensive range of large print and clear print titles.

**Large Print titles are in 16 point Tiresias font as recommended by the RNIB.**

**Clear Print titles are in 13 point Tiresias font and designed for those who find standard print difficult to read.**

### Customer Service

If there is a serious error in the text or layout please send details to feedback@echo-library.com and we will supply a corrected copy. If there is a printing fault or the book is damaged please refer to your supplier.

Printed in the United States
92348LV00007B/13/A